THE YEAR I BECAME ISABELLA ANDERS

JESSICA SORENSEN

The Year I Became Isabella Anders
Jessica Sorensen
All rights reserved.
Copyright © 2015 by Jessica Sorensen
First Paperback Edition: September 2015

ISBN: 978-1517102548

For information: *jessicasorensen.com*

Cover Design by
Okay Creations

Photography by
Perrywinkle Photography

Interior Design and Formatting by
Christine Borgford, Perfectly Publishable

Chapter
ONE

I've always rocked the weirdo gene, and I've mostly been okay with that. But life would be a tiny bit easier if my parents and sister marched to the beat of their own drum, too. Unfortunately, their style is more *Leave it to Beaver* with an edge. My mom is the epitome of a Stepford housewife on crack. She can bake a cake, clean the house, put together a fundraiser for our school, and make sure my sister and I are doing our homework, all while looking perfect.

To most, my dad is the perfect husband and father. He works in the city and is the vice president of a company. He makes a decent salary, like most people who work in the city do, holds a high status in the community, and gives my mother everything she asks for.

Then there's my older sister, Hannah. Growing up, Hannah was the star prodigy of my parents. From preschool up until first grade, she starred in beauty pageants and won so many tiaras and trophies my parents made a special room for them, which basically meant she has two bedrooms. As she got older, she got into modeling and was even in her own commercial for some robotic gadget that was supposed to tease hair to its 'fullest potential'. My parents were always bragging about her at work functions and community get-togethers.

High school is where Hannah really blossomed, according to everyone. She developed an obsession with makeup and fashion, and her confidence and beauty helped her rise to the top social status tier. She became student body president, head cheerleader, and Queen of Sunnyvale, the title handed to one lucky senior who receives a flashy crown, free dinner at the club for a year, the privilege of riding on the float in the Sunnyvale Sunny Days parade, and a scholarship.

Then there's me, the baggy clothes wearing, manga loving, aspiring comic book artist, zombie enthusiast addition to our family. Being different would be fine—there has to be a weirdo in every family—except mine isn't very accepting of people they can't understand, including their own daughter. A junior in high school, my greatest accomplishment is having my own blog that is just a way for me to get all the clusterfuck of weirdness out of my head.

I once beat the entire neighborhood, including the guys, in a free shot competition. But when I do shit like that, it always earns the same reaction from my mother: "You're such a tomboy. When are you going to act like a girl?"

I clock in a lot of time reading, dye my hair an array of colors—today it's green stripes!—and doodle my own comics starring kickass female characters who aren't afraid to be themselves, my attribute I try to live by. Sometimes it's hard, though, trying to find people who 'get me' or whatever. I live in my own little shell as the outcast. Sometimes I feel like I can barely breathe, like the walls are closing in. My worst fear is that I'll die in that damn shell, probably by asphyxiation.

"Why aren't you breathing?" my mom asks me from across the lengthy dinner table.

I hold my breath another few seconds before releasing a deafening exhale. "I was just wondering how long it'd take to die from lack of air." *And if anyone would notice if I dropped dead at the kitchen table.*

She stares at me, unimpressed, then shakes her head and looks over at my dad. "I really don't get her sometimes." She cuts into her chicken, sawing into the meat so violently the knife scrapes against the plate. "No, I take that back. I don't understand her at all."

Hannah snorts a laugh as her manicured nails tap buttons on her phone. "No one does. Just ask anyone at school."

"Hey, some people get me," I argue, stabbing my fork into my salad. "I swear they do."

She glances up at me with her brows arched. "Name one person. And the janitor doesn't count."

"I'm not counting the janitor," I say, chewing on a bite of salad. I've never understood why my sister seems to hate me so much, but ever since we were in grade school, she's made it her mission to torment me as much as she can. "Although, Del's pretty cool."

"Oh, my God, you're a freak," she sneers. "And I know you don't have friends, so don't pretend like they exist."

"Just because the people I hang out with aren't cool enough for you, doesn't mean they don't exist." I'm calm. Perfectly cool. A lazy river on a hot summer day. Because if I'm not—if I lose my shit with Hannah—my ass will be sent to my room without dessert. And I love dessert almost as much as I love manga.

Hannah dramatically rolls her eyes. "You're so lame. At least own that you're a loner and spare yourself the embarrassment of pretending you're not a loser."

I bite my tongue to keep from firing off anything that'll get me into trouble and chant a lovely sweet treat song inside my head.

Oreo cake. Cookie dough ice cream. Strawberry cheesecake.

"You know what?" Hannah sets the phone down on the table, and when she smiles at me maliciously, I know she's about to say something that's going to get me into trouble—that even my sweet treat chant won't save me from. "I take that back. Maybe the janitor can count. I mean, you eat all your lunches in the janitor's closet, right?"

"No," I say through gritted teeth. "And you know I don't, since you pretend to ignore me every day during lunch."

Her grin broadens at the sound of my clipped tone, because she knows she's won—that I'm about to lose my cool. She mouths, *Loser.*

A slow breath eases from my lips, and then I stuff my mouth full of chicken.

Snickers. Chocolate chip cookies. Funnel cake—

"Oh wait!" Hannah exclaims with a laugh. "I do remember you hanging out once or twice with that freak who always wears mismatched shoes. But I think she's into girls . . ." She taps her finger against her lip. "Wait, is she your girlfriend?"

I can't control it any longer. I swallow the chicken and drop the fork. "Leave Lana out of this. She's a nice person, unlike you." I drop my voice and utter the nickname I know she hates, "Super Bitch."

"Mom!" Hannah whines, slamming her palm onto the table and sending the salt and pepper shakers toppling over, along with my mother's wine. "Isa called me a bitch."

My father and mother stare at the mess on the crisp linen tablecloth then my mother glares at me.

"Isabella, you can go to your room now," she says as she scoots back from the table.

"But I didn't do anything." I try not to sound whiney, because it'll only piss her off more. "Well, not anything that she didn't do."

"And you don't get any dessert," she says, ignoring my protests as she strides to the kitchen door.

"I'm really sorry," I tell her as calmly as I can, "but she did call me a loser."

"You're such a liar." Hannah flips her blonde hair off her shoulder and flashes me a smirk when no one's looking.

My mother looks at my father in that way that says *you take care of her* then she slams her palm against the door and whisks out of the room.

"Isabella, your mother said to go to your room, so go to your room." He speaks robotically, as if he rehearsed the words. He avoids eye contact with me, staring at his plate. "And no dessert."

He rarely looks at me, and I haven't ever figured out why. I asked him about it once, but he pretended like he didn't hear me and hurried out of the room, leaving me to draw my own conclusions. My very overactive imagination has conjured up quite a few borderline crazy ideas, ranging from him thinking I look like a hideous beast, to him fearing I secretly possess the superpower to change anyone who makes eye contact with me into a human corpse.

Knowing there's no way my father's going to cave on my punishment—since we've been in this same situation at least a hundred times—I stand up. "Okay."

"And apologize to your sister," he adds, still staring at his chicken like it's the most fascinating thing in the world.

Only when I turn my back to Hannah do I mutter, "Sorry." Otherwise, her smirk will drive me bat shit crazy.

As I'm walking out of the room, my mother returns with a towel to clean the mess up, along with a platter of red velvet cupcakes.

"Why are you still here?" she asks me as she sets the platter down at the end of the table. "I told you to go to your room."

With a heavy sigh, I bid farewell to the cupcakes and leave the dining room, trying to convince myself they probably taste like burnt cardboard, even though my mother's won ribbons for her fan-freakin'-tastic cupcakes.

An hour later, I'm sprawled across my bed surrounded by homework, my sketchbook, and a few of my favorite novels. My Chemical Romance is playing from the stereo, and my balcony doors are open, letting a warm May breeze blow inside. I'm still trying to convince myself that my parents don't hate me. That all their anger and bitterness toward me is simply because they don't understand me. That their partialness to my sister has nothing to do with me. But it's hard when my dad won't even look at me, and every time my mother speaks to me, it's either to ground me or to tell me what a disappointment I am.

I lie in bed lost in my thoughts until my belly grumbles. God, I wish I could at least have just a taste of those red velvet cupcakes. But if I'm caught sneaking into the kitchen, my butt will be grounded. It might be worth it, because seriously, my body's about to have a lack-of-sugar conniption fit.

Ugh!

I roll off my bed and do an awesome zombie impression as I crawl across my floor toward my dresser. "Must . . . get . . . sugar . . ."

When I reach the dresser, I hoist myself to my feet and raid the top drawer for some old Halloween candy I stashed there months ago. I find a half eaten bag of jellybeans and a half eaten chocolate bar that doesn't have a wrapper, and I devour both of them.

Turns out the chocolate bar has the gross addition of almonds. I instantly dry heave, realizing why the candy bar was only half eaten to begin with.

"Gross!" I search for a trashcan to spit it out, but I have no clue where mine ended up, so I trip out onto the balcony and spit out the mouthful of candy over the edge.

It takes me about two seconds to realize what a stupid idea this was for three different reasons:

1. My sister is hanging out in the driveway, which is right below my window.

2. The chocolate I just spit out has landed on her head.

3. She's talking to our neighbor, Kyler Meyers.

Kyler Meyers. What can I say about him other than he's gorgeous, popular, the star quarterback, and smart. Like, he takes AP classes and has a 4.0 GPA kind of smart. I'm also in love with him, have been since I was eight years old and he stopped Hannah's ring of minions from picking on me during recess.

"Hey, just leave her alone," he said when he stumbled across us at the playground.

They had me trapped on the top of the slide and were threatening to push me down it. It wouldn't have been a big deal except there was a giant mud puddle at the bottom. Somehow, Hannah had managed to scare all the rest of the kids away, so no one was around to witness what was about to go down. Even the recess monitor was MIA.

Hannah had crossed her arms and raised her brows at Kyler. "Why're you sticking up for her, Kyler? She's a loser." She stepped toward him and batted her eyelashes. "How about you just go back to playing football with your friends and leave us alone."

Kyler glanced at me then around the empty playground. For a moment, I thought he was going to bail, but then he stepped around Hannah and her friends and offered me his hand. "Come on, Isa."

I took his hand and he helped me to my feet. When they'd chased me up here, I'd fallen down and scraped up my knees, but I hardly felt the pain as he held my hand and guided me off the playground.

He only let go of my hand when we were a safe distance away from them. "Are you okay?"

Unable to find my voice, I nodded.

"You should try to stay away from her," he said, looking over his shoulder at Hannah and her crew, who had targeted a new victim.

"Okay." I managed to get one word out and was super proud of that.

He offered me a smile before heading back to the field to play football with his friends, oblivious to how much his good deed meant to me. It was the first time someone had stuck up for me. Ever. And I've been in love with him ever since.

I know my crush won't ever go anywhere, but I guess I'm a glutton for punishment. Deep down, I get that I'm not really in love with Kyler, especially since sometimes he does things that make me hate him. But in love sounds so much less porn star-ish than *in lust*.

The playground isn't the only time he's done something nice for me, though. There's so much more to my in lust crush than that.

When I was in eighth grade, he gave me a rose on Valentine's Day.

"Hey, Isa, I have something for you," he said as he jogged across the middle school parking lot toward me.

I paused when he said my nickname and gaped at him spastically with half a brownie in my mouth. He was a year older than I was, and I couldn't figure out why he was talking to me. Not only was I Hannah's loser younger sister, but I was in middle school and he was in high school.

"Happy Valentine's Day." He stuck out his hand, and his fingers were wrapped around the stem of a red rose.

I cautiously glanced from the rose to him then gulped the brownie down. "Is this a trick?"

Chuckling, he brushed his brown hair out of his eyes. "Why would I ever want to trick you, Isabella? I have no reason to."

My insides quivered at the sound of my name leaving his lips. The last time he had any social interaction with me was when I was in the third grade and he stopped some of his friends from picking on me, including Hannah.

My gaze darted around the mostly vacant parking lot as I searched for a blonde-haired girl hiding out somewhere, laughing her ass off. "Did my sister put you up to this?"

He swiftly shook his head. "I swear to God it's not a trick. I just wanted to do something nice."

I still didn't take the rose, worried the moment I accepted his gift, my sister would show herself and laugh at me. Knowing her, she'd probably have her Super Bitchy

Cheer Pod People with her, who'd be ready to take pictures of my mortification.

"Isa." He dipped his head to make eye contact with me, not because I'm super short—I'm actually above average height—but he's like one-step-away-from-not-making-the-parking-garage-clearance tall. "I swear to you this is just one neighbor giving another neighbor a gift with no tricks attached."

A neighborly gift? I almost frowned. But it was a completely selfish, Hannah-like reaction, so I sucked it up, took the rose, and even managed a smile. "Thanks."

He smiled, and my heart did an Irish tap dance. "You're welcome." He didn't leave right away, and it seemed like he wanted to say more. "Hey, so I have to ask you for a favor." He paused, hesitant. "And you can totally say no, but . . . I really need to work on my free shot for tryouts next season, and since you won that contest and were pretty badass, I thought you and I could practice together. Maybe you could teach me a few pointers."

Is Kyler seriously asking me to help him improve his basketball skills? I wasn't sure how I felt about that. On one hand, I was excited that I had an opportunity to spend time with him. On the other hand, it made me feel like he saw me as one of the guys.

"Sure," I replied with a small smile.

"Thanks." He looked relieved. "Wanna meet at my house tomorrow morning?"

I nodded and he threw me another smile before he turned around and headed toward the football field, located between the middle school and high school.

I stared down at the rose, wondering what the gesture meant—if it meant anything—and spent the next couple of weekends obsessing about every other gesture he did during our practices. Like when he brought me a doughnut or we spent a couple of hours after practice watching a movie. Part of me wonders if he was just being friendly, while another small part of me hoped it meant more.

He even opened up to me a time or two.

"Sometimes I feel like I have to be good all the time—because that's how everyone expects me to be," he muttered after his dad had come home and spent over a half an hour critiquing Kyler while he made basket after basket.

"I'm sure no one expects you to be that way," I said as we sat on his porch steps, drinking lemonade, our clothes soaked with sweat. "No one can be good all the time."

"Yeah, I know." He scratched his arm, staring at the driveway. "But sometimes it feels like the whole school doesn't see it that way. Like I have to be that guy who takes the team to the championships, who gets good grades, who's happy all the damn time, even when things get shitty. My parents expect that too." His hand fell to his lap and he caught my gaze from out of the corner of his eye. "My dad especially. Sometimes it feels like he's trying to live his dreams through me. Sometimes I wish I could just stop."

"Stop being that guy?"

"Stop being the guy who's happy all the time and just be normal."

"Normal is overrated," I mumbled. "Trust me."

"Yeah, maybe. But I'll never know, since I've never felt like anything about my life is normal." He sighed tiredly then shook his head. "You probably think I'm a douchebag, sitting here complaining about my perfect life."

"You're fine. It's okay to complain about life. Everyone gets tired of being who they are at some point." I picked at my fingernails. "And it's okay to change. You know, if you really want to."

He only nodded with his brows furrowed, like the idea greatly confused him. Then he released a breath and leaned back on his elbows. "Thanks for being such a great listener." Then he leaned over and did something amazing. He kissed me on the corner of my lips. "You're so much different than anyone else I know. I feel like I can be myself when I'm around you."

His words meant a lot to me, but the kiss damn near caused me to stop breathing. It was more than just magical. It was out-of-this-realm amazing. The problem was once he got better at free shots, we stopped practicing, and our movie/doughnut/heart-to-heart time ended too. Kyler went back to being the perfect popular guy everyone expected him to be. Yeah, he still smiled and waved to me whenever he saw me, and talked to me during school sometimes, but that was about as far as our friendship ever went. He still sometimes sticks up for me, though, when someone is harassing me at school.

"What the hell was that?" Hannah combs her fingers through her hair then her face pinches in disgust as she stares at the chocolate in her hand. "Oh, my God! Is that bird shit?!"

"Um," Kyler hesitantly glances up at me, and then his gaze drops to her hand. "It could be," he says, even though he witnessed me spit out the chocolate.

He glimpses up at me and we exchange a look. I know he won't rat me out. He's not like that. He's still that nice guy, who wins championships and gets good grades—the guy who everyone loves and who I know secretly wishes he didn't have to be. Although, I sometimes wonder if he still wants to be different. Over the years, he's seemed to grow into his position as being the popular guy everyone loves.

"Isa!" Hannah screeches from the driveway, jerking me away from one of my favorite memories. "Are you listening to me?"

"I wasn't, but now I am," I say, blinking at her.

She grunts, stomping her foot again. "Did you just spit something in my *hair*?"

Call it payback for that stunt she pulled at the dinner table, but honestly, I don't feel that bad.

"Sorry, but the candy had almonds in it and I panicked." I shrug. "I really hate almonds."

"Oh, my God! You're such a freak!" She stomps her feet several more times, throwing one of her infamous Beauty Queen Tantrums.

I feel sickly satisfied when Kyler covers his mouth with his hand to hide his laughter.

"I'm going to get you back for this," she threatens, crossing her arms and giving me her notorious death glare. "Just wait. When I get done with you, even the janitor's closet isn't going to be safe."

"Hey, calm down." Kyler touches her arm. "It's just candy. I'm sure it'll wash out. And Isa didn't mean to. I saw the whole thing. It was an accident."

I kinda wish I really was a zombie, so I could have a legit excuse to shimmy down the railing and gnaw off her arm he's touching.

Hannah takes a few breaths with her eyes narrowed on me, and then she spins toward Kyler, plastering on a plastic smile. "Wait for me while I go wash my hair. Then we can leave for the party."

"Sure. I'll just go shoot some hoops in my driveway or something." He backs down the driveway toward the end of the fence.

Only when he turns his back to us does Hannah lock

her glare back on me. *You're dead,* she mouths.

Eventually she'll make due on her threat, probably at school, when I least expect it. God, how I wish UW was farther than a ten minute drive and she had to go live at college. But nope, she's staying here, at least for a while.

Le sigh. *Story of my life.*

I probably should be majorly concerned over what she's going to do to me, but honestly, my reputation at school can't get any worse. So, I focus on something better, something that'll cheer me up.

My attention wanders to Kyler as he rounds the fence, but my smile plummets when I notice him checking out Hannah. It's his one fault and something I don't get. Yeah, I know she's beautiful, curvy, has long blonde hair, and dresses like a girl, but back in grade school, he seemed disgusted with her. Sometimes he still does, like the time she tripped Jane Tribloton at a pep rally in front of the entire school. Kyler went and helped Jane up, and then I caught him chewing out Hannah in the hallway later on in the day. Those moments remind me of the Kyler I first fell for. But then there's this other side, the one cracked out on guy hormones.

I frown as Kyler continues to check out Hannah. God, she'd swoon herself to death if she knew he was drooling over her ass like he is. She's been trying to get him to ask her out for the last month, ever since her breakup with The Brad—a nickname he gave himself. While Kyler and Hannah aren't officially a couple, they spend a lot of time together. If they do start dating, I'll have to gouge my eyes out so I don't have to witness them making out. Of course, if he actually starts dating my sister, I just might be able to finally get over this silly little crush I have on him.

"Isa, are you okay?" Kyler shouts as he bounces a

THE YEAR I BECAME ISABELLA ANDERS   15

basketball in his driveway while looking in the direction of my balcony.

I shrug. "Yeah. Sure."

"She's always so hard on you," he says, jumping to make a shot. As he moves, his grey t-shirt rides up just enough to give me a sneak peek at those superhero abs I know he has hiding under there.

"Who, my sister?" I ask distractedly as I discreetly check him out.

Stop staring at him, for the love of God.

The ball swishes through the net, and he turns back to me, smiling adorably. "Yeah. I mean, I like her and everything, but she's nice to me. With you, she always seems so . . ." He seems to be searching for the right word.

"Bitchy. Vile. Or how about plotting-my-death-off-the-rocker-Norman-Bates kind of crazy," I offer, resting my arms on the railing.

"Well, I was going to say intense, but those work too." He's trying really hard not to smile.

"Can I ask you a question?" I dare ask, despite the inner voice screaming at me to keep my trap shut.

"Sure." He offers me an easygoing grin.

"Why do you like her? I mean, she's so mean . . . and you're so . . ." I stop myself from saying nice, because I'm uncertain how he'll react.

"I don't know. I just . . ." He glances at the door to my house then rubs the back of his neck, looking really uncomfortable. "Isa, I don't really feel comfortable talking to you about this."

Give me a crown, people, because I just took the title for Most Super Awkward Girl Ever.

Thankfully, the side door of his two-story house swings open and out walks Kai, Kyler's younger brother, who's a junior in high school like me.

He's not wearing a shirt—he usually isn't—his boxers are sticking out of his black cargo shorts, and his light blond hair is smashed on one side, as if he just woke up. The whole sleepyhead, rebellious look he's rocking is a recent change, as well as the people he's started hanging out with, the stoner kids—labeled as such for wearing dark clothing, eating a lot of junk food, and their overall don't-give-a-shit attitude. At least, that's what everyone calls them, although I have yet to see any of them smoking pot. If that were the case, then I'd be a pothead, since the description fits me, too.

"Hey, what's up?" Kai gives a chin nod to Kyler as he closes the door behind him.

"Not much," Kyler says to his brother as he picks up the basketball. "I'm thinking about heading to a party."

"Which one?" Kai asks, stuffing a spoonful of cereal into his mouth.

He shrugs, dribbling the ball against the concrete driveway. "I think one of Hannah's friends is having one."

He chokes on a laugh and spits out a mouthful of cereal. "Sounds like tons of fucking fun." Sarcasm drips from his tone.

"It won't be that bad." Kyler lifts his arms up to shoot another basket.

"It'll be a bunch of dumbass cheerleaders and jocks," Kai says, setting his bowl down on the porch railing.

"I don't know what your problem is." Kyler walks backward toward the grass to collect the ball. "You used to be one of those," he makes air quotes, " 'dumbass jocks', too, before you decided you were too good for everyone."

"That's not what quitting the team was about," Kai replies in a clipped tone. "So stop talking about shit you know nothing about."

"Then what was it about?" Kyler challenges as he scoops up the ball and tucks it under his arm.

Kai shrugs, picking up his bowl, looking pissed off. "Who cares?"

"Whatever, man." Kyler's gaze bores into Kai, like he expects him to cave. "You know everyone thinks you're into drugs now."

Kai lifts his shoulders and shrugs again. "That's their problem. Not mine."

"I'm starting to wonder if they're right."

Kyler sounds more aggravated than I've ever heard him. And trust me, I've eavesdropped on his conversations a lot, so I would know.

They argue for a few minutes longer, acting completely like night and day. Kyler and Kai may be brothers, but they sure don't act like it. Yeah, Kai is equally as gorgeous, in a dangerous, bad boy, let-me-stun-you-with-my-smoldering-eyes kind of way. Up until about six months ago, he used to be almost as good of a football as Kyler is, and nearly as popular. He even flirted and checked out Hannah sometimes. But then one day he did a complete one-eighty, quit the team, and started spending a lot of time ditching school. I always thought it was odd that Kai was the one who went the route Kyler once wanted—well, in terms of changing. I'm not really sure Kyler ever wanted to become a rebellious bad boy.

The one thing that remained Kai, though, is he's really intense, to the point where looking him in the eye can actually be terrifying for some. And for some girls, exhilarating. For me, not so much, because unlike a lot of people, I know there's a dorky side to Kai, who thinks he's funny and who reads comics.

"Believe whatever you want." Kai backs toward the porch, shrugging off Kyler. "Have fun at your lame-ass party."

Kyler dribbles the bejesus out of the ball. "Whatever. Avoid the problem, like you always do." Another slam of the ball. "Cause more problems between Mom and Dad."

Kai seems oddly satisfied by the fact his brother is annoyed with him, and a smile touches his face as he spins for the door. Right before he walks inside, though, he looks over his shoulder at me.

I should probably duck for cover, since I've been caught eavesdropping red-handed. If it had been Kyler, I'd be so mortified that I'd probably bolt back to my room. But with Kai . . . well, he and I sorta have this thing going on, ever since seventh grade. Not a relationship type of thing or anything. It's more like a 'he teases me and annoys the crap out of me' thing. I don't know why he's so persistent about doing it, other than maybe I'm the only person who doesn't get all squirrely every time he looks at them.

I carry his gaze for a beat or two longer, and the smile on his face grows. I narrow my eyes at him and flip him the middle finger, just because I can. He laughs then winks at me before disappearing inside his house.

I check out Kyler one last time before I return to my bed to finish my drawing of Zombie Artist Girl, who looks great in a cape and can behead a zombie like a badass mofo.

But, the second I plant my butt down on the mattress, my bedroom door opens. I prepare myself for an argument with Hannah, figuring it's her coming to chew my ass out for the chocolate incident, but instead, my mom and dad walk in.

I give them both a puzzled look, because they hardly ever step foot in my room, let alone together.

My mom scans all the movie, comic, and band posters

hanging on my black and violet walls then rolls her eyes at one of my sketches, or what she calls my 'coloring book drawings'.

"What a waste of time," she mutters, shaking her head.

I blow out a breath, trying to let her disapproval breeze past me. But that lack of air sensation appears as my lungs tighten and the shell I live in shrinks even more.

"Did you guys need something?" I close my sketchbook to avoid any more of her insults.

Her cold eyes land on me. "Turn the music down. We need to talk."

I look over at my dad, who's staring at the window, his eyes all lost-scared-puppy wide.

Something's up.

"Okay." I tear my attention off my dad as I reach over to turn down my stereo. "What's up?"

She presses a glance at my dad, but his eyes are fastened on the window. "Do you want to tell her? Or should I?" When my father doesn't budge, she huffs, snapping her fingers. "Henry, we agreed to this, so either you can tell her, or I can."

My dad rubs his hand over his head then looks at me. Or, well, the space around me. "Isabella, your mother thinks—" My mom clears her throat, and my father adds, "Your mother and I were thinking that you should live with your grandmother for the summer."

"For the *entire* summer?" I ask, shocked.

"You'll go in a couple of days when school gets out," my mom says, smoothing invisible wrinkles out of her pencil skirt. "And you can return here to finish up your senior year."

The way she words it is confusing, like they're kicking me out but allowing me to come back to finish school.

I'm not sure how I feel about this. "Which grandmother?"

My dad clears his throat. "Grandma Stephy."

I relax a bit. If it would've been Grandma Jane, my mom's mom, then it would've been an entirely different story. The woman criticizes me even more than my mom does, so much that I sometimes refer to her as *Grandma Jane, Isabella Ego Slayer*.

"Okay, I'll go." And hey, it might be good to get a break, if for nothing else than to get away from Hannah and whatever death-to-Isabella tactics she has planned for the summer.

"Of course you'll go, since it's not a choice," my mom snaps. "We didn't come in here to ask you to go. We came in here to tell you that you're going to go. That we need a little bit of a break from your sarcasm, your rudeness, and your," she waves her fingers at my worn-out sneakers, holey, a-size-too-big jeans, and my oversized hoodie—my typical outfit, "whatever the hell this disaster is."

"Honey, easy." My dad glances at me, throwing me off with the brief eye contact. "She's just a kid."

She points a finger at him. "Don't you *easy* me. I've had enough of this," her finger moves to me, "enough of her. And quite frankly, enough of you. I need a break from one of you, so it's either you or her, and I'd really prefer her." She spins on her heels for the door. "This was never part of the deal, and I want it fixed." She storms out of the room.

"What deal?" I ask my dad.

My dad's gaze bounces back and forth between me and the doorway. "Sorry, Isa. I really am," he mutters before rushing away with his shoulders hunched, cowering like a dog with his tail between his legs. He stops in the doorway for a second to say, "Call your grandmother.

She wants to talk to you about taking a trip overseas, if you're up for it. But don't tell you mother; otherwise, she might not let you go do something so . . . fun." Then he hurries out of the room like it's on fire.

I take a few measured breaths then flop onto my bed and hug Mr. Scribbles, a teddy bear my dad won for me at a carnival when I was about five. It was during the one and only birthday he and I spent together. The day had been absolutely magical, full of spun sugar, bright lights, and the chiming of games. I felt like I was floating on clouds until we got back to the house, and my mom yelled at him for over an hour because he missed one of Hannah's beauty pageants. The only way she let him off the hook was when he promised that he would, "never do such a selfish thing again." That was around the same time he stopped making eye contact with me.

I set the bear down and roll over on my stomach, battling back the tears as I work on my comic book drawing. It's one of my personal favorites, mostly because it stars my alter ego, who's much more ballsy than me. I have a sidekick, too, a woman who I sometimes like to pretend is my mom. She treats me fantastically and always tells me, *Great job!* every time I kick ass. I actually draw the woman a lot; she's been stuck in my head for as long as I can remember. Sometimes she even makes appearances in my daydreams, where she takes me to movies, out shopping, and sometimes we just spend the entire day riding the Ferris wheel. She never gets angry with me or makes me feel small and insignificant. She even tells me she loves me.

I wipe a few stray tears from my cheeks and close my sketchbook. I've trained myself pretty well not to get too emotional over the stuff they say to me—especially my mom—but I'm not a super robot immune to such human emotion. I'm a seventeen-year-old girl who knows she's not the best daughter, who, yeah, tests her parents' patience a lot, and probably spends way too much time drawing comics and watching cartoons. But I still want to, just once, hear them say *I love you.*

My dad said it a couple of times when I was younger, but it's been a while. And I'm almost sure my mom has at some point, but it's been so long I can't remember. I've started to fear maybe there's something wrong with me that makes me so unlovable.

"It's not you. It's them," I try to convince myself as I curl into a ball with the teddy bear.

But as I lie by myself in my room, something I do almost every day, I have to wonder if I'm wrong.

Maybe there really is something wrong with me.

Chapter
TWO

My dad was right. My Grandma Stephy does want me to go overseas with her.

"Are you sure you don't mind if I go with you?" I ask her the next morning before I head to school.

"Why the hell would I?" she asks, being her blunt, doesn't-give-a-shit self. "Besides, if you go, then I'll have someone young and fun to hang out with other than those old biddies."

"Wait? Old biddies? Who are we going with?" I dig through my dresser, looking for a clean t-shirt, but can't find one, so I end up rummaging one out of the hamper.

"The rest of the Sunnyvale Bay Community."

"So a bunch of old people?" My mood deflates. But then I remind myself it doesn't really matter who I'll be going with. Anything is better than being home.

"Hey, I'm not old!" she argues. "Not even close."

"Sorry." I grab my sneakers from the closet. "I didn't mean you. I know you're not old."

"Good girl," she says. "Now, make sure to pack light. I don't want to be hauling around a bunch of clothes, shoes, and shit we don't need. Makes the suitcases too heavy and hurts my back."

"All right, I will. And thanks again for letting me go with you."

"I'm glad you're going, Isa. We're going to have a lot of fun."

After I say goodbye, I hang up, change my shirt, and put on my sneakers. Then I run a brush through my tangled hair, pick up my bag, and head for the door to go to school, wondering what I've gotten myself into. Going on a trip overseas sounds like a blast, and I can handle going with Grandma Stephy. But going with an entire a group of senior citizens . . . I wonder if I'll be the only teenager there.

Oh, well. Doesn't really matter. I don't exactly have a choice. So, I might as well make the best of the situation. And hey, maybe the break from my family will be a good opportunity to do some soul searching without the worry of being scrutinized.

Over the next few days, I finish final exams during the day while packing my bags at night. I spend a whole five minutes saying goodbye to the few friends I have, but I'm not super close with anyone, and the see-ya-laters are a depressing reminder of just how much of a loner I am.

My parents go back to barely speaking to me, although my sister's been overly chatty. She even convinced her Cheer Posse to do a cheer for me while I was walking across the gym, and then they laughed at me. I still don't really understand why they were laughing.

They were the ones who looked like morons bouncing around with pom-poms and chanting a cheer, where they rhymed dork with joke and spelled my name with a z.

By the time I'm actually loading up my stuff to go to my grandma's, I'm stoked to be getting away for a while, even if it's on a three-month trip with people five times my age.

"Do you have everything you need?" my dad asks me as he loads the last of my suitcases into the back of our SUV.

I nod, staring at the front window of the house, where my mother is watching me with her arms crossed. "I should probably go say goodbye to her, right?"

He shuts the trunk of the car, steps back, and tracks my gaze to the window. "Maybe you should just wave goodbye. Might be easier, since she's so upset."

"But why is she even upset with me? I didn't really do anything but argue with Hannah."

"That's not what this is about." He struggles for words and to look at me, but finally, he manages to do both. "It's just hard for her sometimes, but I think this trip might help . . . ease some of the tension." He pats my arm, causing me to jump, and he jerks back. "Sorry." He massages the back of his neck, squirming. "I'm just going to go tell her we're leaving then we'll hit the road. We can even get some ice cream on our way out, if you want."

Normally, I'd be all over the offer to stop for sugar, but even cookie dough ice cream can't melt the fact that my own mother doesn't want to say bye to me.

I slump against the back of the SUV. "Okay. Sure."

He hesitates, his lips parting like he's about to say something. But then he decides against it, rushes up the driveway, and hurries inside the house.

A few seconds later, my sister pulls up in her shiny

silver Mercedes. She honks her horn, scaring the living daylights out of me before she turns off the engine and climbs out.

"A little jumpy, aren't ya?" she sneers as she bumps the door shut with her hip. "I guess I'd be, too, though, if I was getting kicked out of the house."

"I'm not getting kicked out of the house," I say. "I'm just going to visit Grandma."

"Keep telling yourself that, but I seriously wouldn't be surprised if I never saw your pasty face again." She slings the handle of her purse over her shoulder and starts up the driveway, but pauses and shoots me a smirk. "Oh! I completely forgot to tell you the fabulous news."

She may think she's perfect, but she's not, I try to convince myself. *See the lipstick on her teeth? It looks like she fed on someone's blood. Plus, her hair looks kind of frizzy today, like she stuck her finger in a socket.*

I shake my head at myself. Who am I kidding? She's perfect. Albeit evil, but still, that doesn't seem to count for much with the people I go to school with.

"Kyler and I are officially a couple." She flips her hair off her shoulder, her smirk growing.

"Huh?" I blink at her. What the hell did she just say?

"Kyler and I are a couple." She enunciates each word. "You know, our next door neighbor, who you've been in love with since forever."

My jaw nearly smacks the concrete. "I-I'm not in love with K-Kyler."

"Oh, please. Everyone knows you've been in love with him since he gave you that stupid rose, which, FYI, was a pity gift."

I want to tell her she's wrong. That I was in love—in lust—with Kyler before that, but that would only confirm her accusation that I'm in love with her new boyfriend.

Oh, my God.

Reality slaps me hard across the face, and my stomach twists. It's not like Kyler hasn't dated anyone before. He's had a few steady girlfriends over the last couple of years, and I've always handled that pretty well. But dating Hannah? God, I knew it might be coming, but deep down I think I was in denial, naïvely believing that Kyler would never date a person who is so ugly on the inside.

"He told everyone the next day he gave you the rose because he felt sorry for you." She covers her mouth when my expression sinks. "Oh, my God, you didn't know that? That's so sad." She lowers her hand. "And tragic. I can't believe you'd ever think he'd love someone like you." Her face twists with disgust. "That godawful hair. Seriously, who puts green in their hair? And those clothes," she shudders, "so gross."

"I'm not in love with Kyler," I argue, breathing in and out, trying to fight back the waterworks. "So, none of what you're saying matters."

Let her words roll right off you. She's not a good person.

"You're such a bad liar. Always have been." She turns her back on me and strolls toward the door, her four-inch heels clicking against the sidewalk. "And for the record, Kyler's an amazing kisser." She giggles to herself before going inside and shutting the door.

I ball my hands into fists. "One of these days, I swear to God I'm going to . . ." I trail off as I feel someone watching me.

I glance over at the Meyers' house then internally cringe. Kai is sitting on the back porch, staring at me. He's wearing a pair of black board shorts, his hair looks damp, and those intense eyes of his are practically boring a hole into my head.

Shit. Did he just hear all of mine and Hannah's

conversation? Fuck it. Does it really matter? I'm sure Hannah's already pretty much told Kyler I'm obsessed with him.

"You're going to what?" Kai ask with his head cocked.

"Huh?" My stomach flips with my nerves. If he does know I like Kyler, he's never going to let me live it down. Because that's what Kai has been doing for the last six months, teasing me whenever he sees a good opportunity.

His lips quirk, like he's fighting back a laugh. "I was just wondering what you were going to do to your sister." He nods his head at the door. "You never finished your thought, and I'm really curious what your twisted mind was going to come up with this time."

My lip curls, because I'm not sure if he's teasing me or being serious. I never do with him. "I didn't finish my thought, because I was trying to make it really good. Like sickly morbid and full of torture. But thanks for ruining my train of thought."

He chuckles. "I'm going to miss this."

My brows drip. "Miss what?"

He raises his head, grinning, and for some reason that only pisses me off more. "Our lovely little chats."

I stare at him, unimpressed. "Is that what you call torturing the nerdy next door neighbor?"

He presses his hand to his chest. "I've never tortured you. That's your sister's thing. Not mine. I've always been nice to you."

A disdainful laugh escapes my mouth. "Like the time you told me the stripes in my hair made me look like a rainbow?"

"Hey, rainbows are cool." He seems totally amused and has his smoldering let-me-bind-you-in-place gaze going on.

It's driving me absolutely crazy, and I become

desperate to win our little argument. "Okay, how about the time you ate my science fair project?"

"Hey, who puts chocolate on their science fair project?" He gapes at me. "Seriously, that was your own damn fault."

Okay, he has a point. The Chocolate Volcano Project was kind of a disaster.

"How'd you know I'm leaving?" I change the subject, wandering toward the fence.

"You mean besides the suitcases you just loaded up in the back of the SUV?" he questions, cocking his brow. But underneath the surface, he abruptly grows uneasy, fiddling with the leather bands on his wrists.

"You heard it from someone." I eye him over with suspicion. "I can tell, because you got all squiggly."

He rolls his eyes, like I'm being ridiculous, but then surrenders. "Fine, your sister's been telling everyone."

"That I'm leaving?" My brows knit. "Why would she do that?"

He scratches at the back of his neck, looking everywhere but at me. "Um . . . well . . . she's been telling everyone that you're being admitted to a mental institution, but I know that's not true."

Invisible pins stab at my skin. I don't want to hate my sister . . . I really don't . . . but I kinda hate her right now.

"Why'd she say I was going?" My voice sounds so hollow.

"That doesn't matter." He rises to his feet, steps off the porch, and strides over to the fence. "Where are you going, though?"

"Overseas with my grandma, which probably sounds lame, but I'm actually looking forward to it."

"It doesn't sound lame at all."

"Not even the going-with-the-grandma part?"

He shakes his head, waving me off. "Nah, grandmas can be cool sometimes. Is yours?"

"She's like the Queen of Cool Grandmas. Seriously. She's the one who taught me how to drive. And I'm talking, like floor-your-car-to-the-max kind of driving. She taught me how to swim too, in a pool that was closed. We had to sneak in through this hole in the fence. She even let me try beer for the first time." I pause, realizing something. "You know, without her, I might have ended up lacking a lot of necessary life skills. Well, beside the drinking-the-beer part. I don't think that's a life skill."

"Oh, that can be a life skill," he assures me with a devious grin, and I repress one of my own, not wanting to encourage him. "She does sound pretty cool, though."

I bob my head up and down in agreement, fully aware of how lucky I am to be going on this trip with the coolest grandma ever.

"You'll have to post some pictures so I can see all the awesome things you do on this trip," Kai says, squinting against the sunlight.

I snort a laugh. "Oh, Kai, and your silly little jokes. We both know I'm not cool enough for social media."

"That wasn't meant to be a joke." He stuffs his hand into his pocket and retrieves his phone. "But if you're really that anti-social, then I'll give you my number and you can send all of your awesome photos to me. It'll make me feel special too."

I roll my eyes, but give him my number so he can text me his. I don't really think he's going to do it, but two seconds later, my phone vibrates from inside the pocket of my jeans.

"Have fun on your trip. And I mean that, Isa. Have fun. You deserve it, more than anyone." He gives me a strange look as he puts his phone away, like he can't quite figure something out, then swiftly clears his throat. "Yeah, but the whole point of me coming over here was to give you a little advice."

I pull a wary face. "I'm not sure I want to hear your advice."

He offers me one of his infamous sexy, playful pouts. "Why not?"

"Because . . ." I sigh heavy-heartedly when his sexy, playful pout turns into genuine sulking. "Fine. You can give me advice, just as long as it's not an 'It'll Get Better After High School' speech. I don't want to hear any of those. I've heard too many of those kinds of speeches."

"It's not one of those. I promise. Cross my heart and hope to die. Stick a needle through Hannah's eye." He draws an X across his chest, giving me a lopsided grin.

I can't help but grin goofily back at him. "I'm surprised you remember that."

"Of course I remember that. We used to say it all the time."

"Yeah, but that was a long time ago, back when we were actually kind of friends."

An awkward quiet fills the air between us as the past hovers over our heads.

See, once upon a time, Kai and I used to hang out. And not in the way Kyler and I hung out for a few weekends while I helped him improve his free shot skills and he opened up to me once. Unlike Kyler, Kai and I were actually friends. Well, sort of. For most of seventh grade, he walked home with me after school. He always seemed sad about something as we strolled up the sidewalk toward his house. While I could never figure out what had him feeling so blue, I did learn some stuff about him that no one else knew. Like he's secretly into comic books. Likes zombie movies. And listens to 80s punk rock.

During the time we spent together, I always tried to cheer him up—it was the least I could do for him for not being too embarrassed to walk home with me. Sometimes my jokes made him smile. Other times, he seemed too stuck in his head. But even if the walk was filled with quietness, it was nice to have a friend.

After a few months of walking home together, he started hanging out with me on weekends. We'd mostly stay in my room, and sometimes we'd go to the park. I was really starting to believe we had a chance at becoming real, seen-in-public friends. But then came the dreaded day when one of his friends caught us hanging out at the park, and he started making fun of Kai for 'being in love with a loser'. Kai panicked and told his friend I was stalking him, and that was the last time we walked home together.

"My advice was actually about your sister," Kai says, breaking the silence between us. "I was going to say you need to do something to get her to leave you alone. You've put up with her shit for too long."

I stuff my hands into the pocket of my hoodie. "When you say 'do something to get her to leave you alone', are you talking like mafia-style? Or like how Penny Milerford got Nora Benninting to leave her alone by punching her in the face? Because I'm not a mobster, nor a crazed honor roll student who may or may not be on crack."

"Penny isn't on crack. That's just a stupid rumor." His expression hardens as he backs away from the fence. "People need to stop spreading shit around about other people, just because they think something's wrong." He starts up the porch stairs, and I figure our conversation is over until he stops in front of the door and turns around. The intensity pouring out of his eyes startles the crap out of me, because he never directs that kind of look on me. With me, it's always joke-this or joke-that. Look at me. I'm so funny and cute. Yada, yada, yada. "And, Isa. I meant for *you* to do whatever *you* feel you need to do to get her to stop treating you so shitty. Stand up for yourself, okay? She's not any better than you, no matter what she thinks." His crazed look softens.

"Since when are you so anti-Hannah? You used to flirt with her all the time."

That's the thing with both Kyler and Kai. While Kyler is mostly nice to me, and Kai spends a lot of time teasing me, neither of the guys have shown me the attention they've shown Hannah. Over the years, particularly when we all got in high school, both of them have spent a ton of time flirting with her and her friends, checking her out, and trying to get her attention.

"I only flirt with her when I'm bored," Kai says, seeming bored right now. "But I get that she's a bitch. And I haven't liked her since I . . ." He trails off, but I know what he's going to say. *Since I went off the deep end and went all bad boy.* "But anyway, have fun on your trip." He winks at me, going from serious to joking in two seconds flat. "And bring back something super cool for your most awesome, super sexy next door neighbor."

"Huh? Who am I supposed to bring the present back for?" I glance around, pretending to be confused.

His eyes narrow to slits, but he grins. "You know exactly who I'm talking about. The guy who fills up all of your dreams."

"You mean Johny Palerson?" I feign innocence.

He snickers. "I forgot about your little seventh grade crush on that douche." He pauses. "You're still not into him, are you?"

"I'm more into him than my cocky neighbor next door," I quip with a sassy smirk.

His eyes darken as he backs away from me. "You know, if you bring me back a present, it means that's not true. That you do really like me." He winks at me again and walks into the house before I can get another word out.

His advice echoes in my head.

He may joke around a lot with me, but when he gets all serious, he actually gives pretty good advice.

I make a vow to myself right then and there that when I get back from this trip, things will change. I'm not sure how it's going to happen, but if I can survive seventeen years of being picked on, I sure as hell can figure out a way to finally make it stop.

Chapter
THREE

I'm still trying to create an awesome plan on how to get Hannah to respect me, when my dad returns to the car.

"Ready?" he asks me as he fishes the keys from his slacks.

Nodding, I hop into the passenger seat.

My thoughts remain stuck in Awesome Plan Land for most of the thirty-minute drive across town. The only time the quietness is broken is when we stop at the drive-thru to get ice cream like my dad promised, and he asks me what flavor I want.

By the time we pull up to the Sunnyvale Bay Community, I'm still lost on how to make Hannah see me differently. It doesn't seem possible, considering I'm basically trying to figure out a way to get Hannah, The Wicked Wench of the Anders' House, to be nicer to me.

No, I can do this, I tell myself. *I need to be more optimistic. I have a whole three months to figure this all out.*

The Sunnyvale Bay Community looks like an ordinary apartment complex, except all the tenants are fifty-five and over. Grandma Stephy moved here about a year ago after my grandpa passed away from cancer. While my grandpa was a man of few words, he was probably my favorite family member besides Grandma Stephy. Whenever I visited, he'd take me down to the gas station to buy a soda and candy. We'd cruise on the back roads in his old truck, listening to old country singers, mostly Hank Williams and Johnny Cash, with the windows down, even if it was wintertime. He never took Hannah with us. Said she threw too many tantrums. Our drives always made me feel special, like someone actually wanted to spend time with me, like I was more than just Hannah's dorky little sister who no one ever wanted around.

Man, I really miss those days and our drives.

"I'll get your bags if you want to go up," my dad says, interrupting my thoughts as he parks the car.

"Sure. Sounds good. Thanks." I climb out of the car and head up the path to my grandma's apartment.

I knock before opening the door and strolling inside. As I step foot over the threshold, my shoe bumps into Beastie, my grandma's fat, old calico cat, and I fall flat on my stomach.

The cat hisses at me, like the crabby old fart he is.

"Dammit, Beastie," I curse as I roll over onto my back, rubbing the knee I banged against the floor.

He growls and the hairs rise on his back as he scurries at me with his claws out. I scramble to get to my feet, but right as his claw is about to reach my leg, a pair of hands wrap around his belly.

"Now, Beastie, I thought we talked about this." My cousin, Indigo, who's two years older than me, scoops up the cat and lifts him so he's eye level with her. Looking him dead in the eyes, she lectures, "It's rude to trip people then try to eat their faces. You're not a zombie. You're a cat."

Beastie hisses at her in response.

Sighing, she sets him back down on the floor and offers me her hand. "I've been telling Grandma Stephy that she needs to teach him some manners, but she says it's useless, that he's too old and already stuck in his ways."

"She's probably right." When I take her hand, she helps me to my feet. I massage my achy knee. "Don't take this the wrong way, but what're you doing here? I thought you were in New York attending art school."

"I was." She tucks a strand of her blood red hair behind her ear and fiddles with one of her gauges. "Some stuff came up, though, and I had to leave."

"Did you move back home?"

"Nah, my parent's didn't want to," she makes air quotes, "'encourage my dropout behavior'. I think they thought if they didn't let me move back in that I'd go back to school." She rolls her eyes as her hands fall to her sides. "I tried to explain to them that I didn't dropout, that the school decided it was probably for the better if I take a permanent sabbatical. But you know parents. They hear what they want to hear." She glares at Beastie as he hisses at her from underneath the coffee table. "Thankfully, Grandma Stephy took me in until I can figure out what the hell I should do with my life."

I want to ask her what she did to get kicked out of school, but I don't know Indigo that well. Her mother is my father's sister and the two of them rarely speak to one another, other than when we're at family reunions, and even then, the conversation is strictly formal. And my mom refuses to speak to hardly any of my dad's relatives, because she says they act like a bunch of hippies.

All I really know about Indigo is that she's into art and self-expressionism, through painting and with her body. I once heard her call her body a canvas. She has tons of tattoos and several piercings and does all sorts of crazy stuff with her hair, even shaving her head one time.

"So are you looking after Grandma Stephy's house while we're gone?" I ask, stealing a butterscotch from the candy dish.

She shakes her head, flopping down on the floral sofa. "Nah, I'm going with you guys." She kicks her boots up on the coffee table and crosses her legs. "I figure a little trip overseas might lead me down a path to self-discovery."

"Don't let her fool ya with her artsy-fartsy talk," Grandma Stephy says as she enters the living room. She's cut her hair since the last time I saw her, but is still rocking the grey. She's never really dressed very grandmother-ish and is decked out in a pair of rhinestone jeans and a pink t-shirt. "The reason she's going is to see Peter."

"Who's Peter?" I peel the wrapper off the candy and pop the treat into my mouth.

"Some guy she met in New York who I guess lives in London," Grandma Stephy explains as she opens her arms to give me a hug. "But enough about Indigo. I've heard enough about British guys to last me a lifetime. What I really want to hear about is you." She wraps her arms around me and gives me the first hug I've had in months. "How you holdin' up, honey?"

"I'm okay." I hug her back, getting a whiff of hairspray and floral perfume. It makes me smile, because it's so her and it reminds me that I'm here, with her, for the next three months, where maybe I won't feel like such an outcast.

"It's going to be okay," she tells me, patting my back. "Um, thanks." I pull back, sensing something's off. "Is something wrong? You seem a little, I don't know, sad."

She eyes me over. "I was just going to ask you the same question."

Okay . . . what the hell is going on?

"Isabella's fine," my dad insists as he walks in and drops my suitcases on the floor. He locks eyes with Grandma Stephy and gives her a pressing look. "You and I need to talk privately about what to say and what not to say. I know how much you like to run your mouth."

My grandma shakes her head at my dad. "Good grief, sometimes it's hard to believe I raised you."

My dad looks taken aback. "What the hell's that supposed to mean?"

She narrows her eyes at him. "It means you've turned into an asshole over the years you've spent with—"

"Don't you dare bring my wife into this," he warns, his face reddening.

"I wouldn't have to if she didn't . . ." She trails off, glancing at me with worry.

The two of them arguing is nothing new, but the way they keep looking at me, like I've suddenly started glowing neon green and sprouted an eye in the middle of my forehead, is definitely out of the norm.

"Fine. You want to talk privately, then come on." Her voice is cold, her expression hard as she turns and storms down the hallway.

My dad marches after her, fuming mad. Moments later, a door slams shut, but I can still hear their muffled voices.

"What do you think that was about?" I ask, turning to Indigo.

She shrugs with her brows furrowed. "I have no idea." Her eyes light up as she plants her feet onto the floor. "But I know how we can find out. Come on."

I reluctantly follow her as she hurries down the hallway toward where my dad and grandma went. As we near the bedroom door, their voices grow louder and clearer.

"Are they yelling at each other?" I whisper to Indigo as we stop in front of the door.

She nods as she presses her ear to the door. "They've been doing it a lot lately on the phone, too," she whispers. "I'm not sure what it's about, though."

"Can you hear anything?" I whisper, inching closer.

She puts her finger to her lips, shushing me. "I think . . ." She doesn't finish her thought, driving me mad! Mad, I tell you!

I press my ear to the door and listen for myself.

"You have no right to do this," my dad growls, sounding more furious than I've ever heard him, including the time he yelled at me for sneaking a sip of his scotch. "She's not your child."

"Well, she's barely yours with how shitty you treat her," Grandma Stephy barks back. "You hardly know that girl at all."

"That's bullshit. I know her better than you. She's my daughter. Not yours."

"Okay, Mr. Know-It-All. If you know your daughter so well, tell me what her favorite manga book is, or hell, just tell me her favorite book." Silence stretches between them, and she adds, "You don't know shit about your daughter. But I do. I know she draws her own comics, and while I don't always understand them, I know a talented artist when I see one. Did you know she writes her own blog? She's pretty clever, too. Plus, on top of that, she's a straight-A student . . . but I'm sure you know all this already, right?" Sarcasm drips from her voice like thick globs of honey. "I mean, she is *your* daughter."

The silence that follows makes my stomach churn as reality crashes down on me. I always knew my father wasn't that interested in me, but the fact that he has no damn clue what makes me tick hurts like a blow to the jugular.

"You know it's hard for me when it comes to her," my father says, speaking more calmly. "And there's circumstances that—"

"I don't give a shit about the circumstances," she snaps. "When you chose to keep her with you, you chose to be her father. If you couldn't handle what that entailed, then you should've let her come live with me like I offered. But no, you decided to take her in and treat her like shit."

I jerk back from the door. "What the hell?" I say louder than I mean to.

Indigo captures my arm and tows me back down the hallway, making a beeline for the front door. I don't know if my grandma or dad heard me, but the bedroom door is still shut by the time Indigo drags me outside. She only releases me when we've crossed the parking lot and reached the tree area across from the apartment.

"Holy shit." I run my fingers through my hair as I pace back and forth across the grass. "I don't get what just happened. I don't . . . none of this makes sense." I place my hands on my hips and hunch forward as my stomach burns. "Keep me? He chose to keep me . . . I don't understand." I peer up at Indigo, who has a cigarette between her lips and a lighter in her hand. "Do you know what any of that was about?"

She cups her hands around her mouth and lights the

cigarette. "I'm not positive, but I have a few theories," she says, a cloud of smoke circling her face. "But they're just theories based on shit I've heard my mother and father talking about."

Still woozy, I squat down and inhale deeply. "What are the theories?"

"I'm not sure I should tell you," she says, eyeing me warily. "You already look like you're about to hack your guts up."

"I feel like I'm going to hack my guts up."

"Here." She crouches down in front of me and offers me her cigarette.

I scrunch my nose. "I don't smoke."

"I know, but a drag or two might help you chill out."

The smoke burns my nostrils as I take the cigarette from her hands. My fingers shake as I lift the end to my lips and inhale. "Holy shit, that burns," I say through a fitful of coughs as my lungs drown in smoke.

Indigo laughs in amusement as she removes the cigarette from my hands. "Sorry. I probably should've warned you first, but I thought going in blind might make it more exciting for you." She sits down in the grass and takes a few drags as I catch my breath.

Once I no longer feel like a ninja used my lungs as a punching bag, I settle in the grass beside her. "I wanna hear your theories. In fact, I need to hear them; otherwise, I'll come up with my own. And my head is full of all sorts of crazy."

She sighs heavily. "I was hoping the whole smoking thing would distract you from that."

Shaking my head, I pick at the grass. "How can I think of anything else, when it sounds like I was . . . adopted?"

"Is that what you think that was about?" she asks, squinting at the highway in front of us.

"Um, yeah." I massage my temples as my head pulsates. All this time, I knew I didn't quite fit in with my family, that I was an outcast. Different. And yeah, the thought crossed my mind that maybe I was adopted, but the thought was never out of seriousness. "What else could it be?"

She grazes her thumb across the end of the cigarette, scattering ashes all over the grass. "It could be adoption . . . or it could be that maybe your . . ." She looks at me and pity fills her eyes. "Have you ever wondered why your mom treats you like shit?"

"You've noticed that?"

"Isa, everyone who's ever crossed paths with the two of you knows there's tension between you and your mother."

"Tension from her," I point out. "I try to be nice, but she acts like I'm some sort of vile reptile or something."

She puts her cigarette between her lips and smoke laces the air as she dazes off at the highway again. "I have this theory that maybe the reason she's always treated you like shit is because maybe you remind her of a shitty time in her life . . . maybe something shitty your dad did to her that kind of led to the procreation of you."

It takes a second or two to process what she's implying. "Wait . . . you think . . ." I shake my head. "No, there's no way. My dad didn't have an affair . . . he wouldn't do that to my mom. Trust me. He does everything she says, sometimes too much."

Her brows arch. "He wouldn't, huh? Okay, I guess my theory's wrong."

I shake my head, but inside, my wheels are turning. All those times my mother looked at me with such disdain, and sometimes jealousy, are starting to make sense.

"I know this isn't what you want to hear," she says

then mutters, "Although, I don't know why. Your mom's a bitch." She clears her throat. "But you have to admit it kind of makes sense."

I lower my head into my hands. "None of this makes sense. Where did you even get this theory? Did you just pull it out of your ass, or is it based on some sort of legit info?"

"I heard a rumor," she says. "Or, well, I overheard my mom and dad gossiping about your family once, and my mom said something about the other woman, and how it was a good thing your dad didn't leave you with her."

Wide-eyed, I lift my head and gape at her. "How long ago was this?"

She shrugs as she puts the cigarette out in a patch of dirt. "I don't know. Like a few years ago or something."

"Why didn't you ever say anything to me?"

"Isa, this is like the longest the two of us have talk-ed. Usually, at reunions, your family stays in a hotel and spends a whole lot of time sitting around in the corner with your noses stuck in the air like a bunch of snobs."

"My mom makes me do that." It hits me as I say it, like a bull charging straight into my stomach. "Wait. Am I even supposed to call her *mom?*" I push to my feet and pace in front of Indigo, reaching full on crazy panic mode. "Or am I supposed to call her Lynn. Oh, my God, I just realized that my sister's middle name is after my mom's first name, but I'm named after no one. It has to be true." I crouch down again as my legs turn into Jell-O. "I don't even know who my mom is."

"Hey, chill out." She scoots toward me to catch my gaze. "My theory is just a theory. And I should probably tell you that I had a theory that Grandpa was reincarnat-ed into Beastie." She smiles as I blink at her. Wow. She sounds as crazy as . . . well, me. "What? They have the same eyes, okay? And you have to admit it'd be pretty cool if reincarnation existed."

"That mean, old cat isn't Grandpa," I say. "But I get what you're saying. I need to get some answers before I have a meltdown."

"Or you could just skip the meltdown and use this as an opportunity," she suggests with a smile.

"An opportunity for what?"

"To take a self-discovering journey."

"But I already know who I am."

She inspects my outfit with her brows raised. "I'm not sure I agree with you."

I tug on the bottom of my hoodie. "Just because I dress a little different doesn't mean I don't know who I am."

Her head slants to the side as she studies me. "Okay, answer this for me. What's the most exciting thing you've ever done?"

"I don't know." I try to think of something, and it's pretty dang sad how hard it is to come up with anything. "I entered a comic contest once. That was really cool."

"I'm not talking about doing stuff that's cool. I'm talking about stuff that's exciting. Like screaming-at-the-top-of-your-lungs-at-a-concert exciting. Dancing-in-a-room-full-of-people-like-no-one's-watching exciting. Or sporadically taking a trip to nowhere with no plans other than to drive." She smiles as she gets a faraway look in her eyes. "Or like being kissed in the rain by a total stranger, who you have no plans of calling again." She looks at me, grinning. "That one I plan on doing while we're on this little trip."

"How do you know it's exciting if you haven't done it yet?" I ask, tucking my feet under me.

"Oh, Isa, the fact that you ask that means you haven't

nearly experienced enough in your life. Life is all about the experiences, the good ones and the bad ones." She stands to her feet, yanking me with her. "Stick with me, and I promise that'll change."

I *almost* open my mouth to tell her I don't want to change, but then I remember her theory, and my grandma and dad's argument rings loudly in my head. What if Indigo is right? What if my entire life has been a lie? What if the reason my mother—Lynn—has always liked Hannah more is because Hannah's her daughter and I'm not?

"Okay, I can try to do more things that are exciting, but what about the theory?" I ask as we cross the parking lot.

"What about it?"

"How do we find out if it's true?"

She links arms with me. "We're going to do a little researching. And if all else fails, we'll wait until Grandma Stephy gets good and drunk and then get her to spill the beans." She grins deviously. "You know she's a talker when she gets too tipsy. Plus, people tend to get a little crazy when they're on vacation, especially out of the country."

"Grandma Stephy is already a little crazy," I say with a small laugh, but it hurts to smile. Hurts to think.

She chuckles. "Yeah, so just think how crazy she's going to get while we're chilling in London or Paris. After a few glasses of wine and a little pushing on our part, we should be able to get the truth out of her." She pats my arm. "We'll get to the bottom of this. I promise. And we're going to teach you what excitement is."

I nod, silently vowing to go along with the plan. But inside, I'm terrified. Because what if it's true? What if I don't even know who my own mother is?

Chapter
FOUR

A week later, I'm chilling out on the balcony of a very nice hotel room, staring out at the sparkling lights of the Eiffel Tower. I'm half listening to Indigo plot out our plan to weasel the truth out of Grandma Stephy, who's downstairs at the bar having drinks.

Ever since I discovered I might not know who my real mom is, my head's been stuck between reality and daydream land, where my mind creates all kinds of scenarios on where this is all going to go, where I'm going to end up if I find out I've been living a lie. I keep replaying all the times my parents acted strange around me, including when my dad didn't even hug me goodbye before he left Grandma Stephy's.

"Have fun, okay?" he said as he walked toward the front door to leave. "And take care of yourself."

I forced a stiff smile. "Okay."

He gave me an awkward pat on the arm before rushing out of the apartment without even saying goodbye to

Grandma or Indigo.

"It's going to be okay," my grandma said with a tense smile. Then she clapped her hands together and made herself smile for real. "All right, you two. Let's finish packing. We leave really early Monday morning."

And that was that. The last seven days have been filled with packing, driving to the airport with a bus full of older people, taking the twelve-hour flight to Paris, and getting to the hotel. We've been here for over a day, but have spent a lot of time catching up on sleep. But after sleeping for most of the day, I feel super awake right now, even though night just fell.

"I was thinking tonight might be the best night to put our plan in motion." Indigo balances an ashtray on her stomach then kicks her feet up on the railing and takes a drag of her cigarette. "I know we just got here and everything, but I don't think we should waste any time. You're already stressing out way too much as it is."

"I'm not stressed . . . I've just been thinking." I try to focus on her and the conversation. "And which plan are we talking about? The excitement one? Or getting Grandma drunk?" I fan my hand in front of my face to cool off.

In Sunnyvale, June temperatures usually hover in the seventies, maybe the eighties on a super intense day, and the nights bottom to forty. Right now, it's eight o'clock and feels like it's ninety degrees outside.

"We aren't going to get her drunk. We're going to wait until she gets drunk. And we might not have to wait that long." She taps her cigarette against the ashtray. "Dude, did you see all the mini bottles she drank on the plane?"

I giggle. "Yeah, I know. I can't believe she was playing a drinking game with her friends."

"I think it's so cool. I hope I'm that cool when I'm

old." She lowers her feet to the ground, leans forward in the chair, and rests her arms on the balcony railing, staring over the edge at the sidewalk below. "I was talking about your self-discovering journey." She pauses, musing over something while puffing on her cigarette. "I think we should start tonight, but not go too crazy." She seems to be talking more to herself than to me. "We have to ease you into this."

"I know I'm not the most exciting person ever," I say, "but I've done some exciting things. You don't have to go easy on me."

She gives me a sidelong glance. "Careful, Isa. Giving me free reign like that can end up being dangerous."

I roll my eyes. "It's just partying. What's the big deal?"

"I'm not just talking about partying; I'm talking about completely letting go. Of everything." She stares me down, like she's trying to get me to take back what I said. I don't crack. Won't. I've spent way too much of my life doing that, something I've painfully become aware of over the last week. A slow smile curls her lips. "All right, let's do this then." She jumps to her feet, wanders back into the room, and begins rummaging around in her suitcase.

"What are you doing?" I ask as I walk into the room.

"Making you club-worthy," she says as she sorts through her dresses, shirts, and shorts.

I grow nervous as she holds up a tight red dress that looks like it will barely cover my ass. "No fucking way." I shake my head. "I can't wear that."

She frowns. "Why not?"

"Well, for starters . . ." I rack my brain for a reason other than I'll feel like an idiot. "I haven't shaved my legs."

She flicks her wrist, motioning me to get a move on. "Well, hurry up and do it then."

I nervously pick at my fingernails. "I, um, didn't bring a razor."

She looks at me with confusion then suddenly relaxes. "Oh, I get it. You've never done any of this before, have you?"

I cross my arms, feeling absurdly self-conscious. "Done what exactly?"

"Shave. Put on makeup." She shoves the red dress at me. "Dress up."

"I've never really cared about my looks, and I've never really been into girly stuff." I pause, feeling idiotic. "And it's kind of hard, you know, to ask my mom—Lynn—to show me how to put on makeup and all that fun stuff, when I know she'll probably just laugh at me and tell me how ridiculous I am to think that'll help my looks."

Like she did the one and only time I asked her to buy me a dress. I was twelve, and it was for the seventh grade dance. I thought I'd dress up, since I heard most of the girls were.

Lynn laughed at me when I asked. "Don't be ridiculous. You'd look hideous in a dress," she said.

I fought back the tears. "I think I should try to dress up. I mean, everyone else in my grade is."

She turned to me with a dead serious expression on her face. "Isabella, I'm going to tell you something that you're not going to like hearing." She hesitated, almost as if she was backing out. "You're too gangling and homely to be dressing up. You should just stick to the baggy jeans and hoodies. It suits your body type better."

As I recollect the memory, I wonder if that was the starting point to my baggy jeans and hoodie obsession.

Sure, I wore them before, but not because I felt like I had to. I just didn't know how to put together an outfit. Plus, they were comfortable to wear while I was playing basketball.

After Lynn told me that, I felt as if I had to dress in baggy clothes, like I wasn't good enough to dress nice.

What if that's the real reason I do a lot of things? What if my general weirdo-ness was created around things my mom—Lynn—said to me. Like when she told me no one wanted to be friends with me because I was too strange. What if I stopped trying to make friends, because I believed no one would want to get to know weirdo, freak I was led to believe I was?

Pity briefly flashes in Indigo's eyes, but the look swiftly vanishes as determination fills her expression. She strides across the room, opens the mini fridge, and grabs a bottle of wine. Using an opener, she removes the cork then takes a swig straight out of the bottle.

God, if Lynn were here, she'd have a fit with the lack of class Indigo is showing right now.

When I hesitate, Indigo says, "No one's around. We don't need to be classy."

"That's not why I'm hesitating." Sighing, I grab the bottle, take a drink, and then give the wine back to her.

She sets the bottle aside then grabs my arm and pulls me toward the bathroom door.

"What are we doing?" I ask as I hurry after her.

"I'm giving you a little lesson. But take notes, because I'm only going to do this once. You can't find out who you are if I'm trying to do it for you."

Two hours later, I'm walking down an overly packed sidewalk with smooth legs and tweezed eyebrows, wearing a red dress I can barely breathe in.

"Come on, Isa," Indigo says, motioning me to move

quicker as she walks a ways in front of me. "If you keep walking this slow, the clubs are gonna be closed by the time we get there."

"I'm trying." I shuffle after her, trying not to roll my ankles. "These heels suck, though."

She slows to a stop at a street corner and sighs as she leans down to untie her boot. "Come on, take them off and I'll trade shoes with you."

I stop beside her and grab the street post to get my balance. "I thought you said heels weren't your thing." Which really confused me, since she packed six pairs.

"I said most of the time they weren't my thing." She slips her foot out of the boot and unties the other one. "It doesn't mean I never wear them."

We exchange shoes and I feel ten times better in the clunky boots. "I think I'm a boots kind of girl for sure."

"I agree." After Indigo slips the heels on, she does a little spin in her dress. "How do I look?"

"Amazing," I say as I finish tying the boots. "I like how the flowers on the shoes match your hair."

"Me too." She studies me with her head cocked to the side. "God, you look so great. It's amazing what a little eyeliner and lip-gloss can do. Well, that, and my ever-so-awesome talent."

I stand up, self-consciously tugging at the hem of the dress. "I honestly feel kind of silly. Like I'm trying to play dress up or something." My gaze sweeps over the crowd of people walking around us. "I feel like everyone thinks I'm an impostor."

She shakes her head with a smile on her face. "Trust me, Isa. No one thinks you're an imposter." She grabs my hand and pulls me with her as she moves with the crowd again.

We walk for what feels like hours, taking in all the

closed stores, the bars, the Arc de Triomphe, and the twinkling lights of the Eiffel Tower.

"Let's go up there," she says as we gawk up at the tower that stretches to the night sky.

"I thought we were going to a club?" I ask as I rush to keep up with her.

"We can go to a club anytime!" she shouts over the music playing from a street band. "Going up there," she tips her head up toward the sky, "now *that's* an once-in-a-lifetime excitement."

When we reach the ridiculously long line, I head toward the end. But Indigo has other ideas and starts searching the line for cute guys who will let us cut in front of them. It takes her three tries to find a couple of guys who even speak English. They let us get in line in front of them then Indigo spends the next half-hour flirting with one of them, while I stand there awkwardly.

"You look nervous," one of the guys whispers in my ear, causing me to jump. "Are you afraid of heights?"

"Um, yeah, sure." I pretend that's the reason I have goosebumps sprouting across my skin, when really it's the guys, the social interaction, the dress—everything, really.

He slings an arm around my shoulders. "Don't worry. I'll protect you." He flashes me a dimpled grin. "I'm Jay, by the way, but you can call me your protector."

I resist an eye roll. *Seriously, dude, those lines can't possibly work.* Then I pause, realizing, *Holy shit, this guy is hitting on me.* While I'm flattered, I have absolutely no interest in Protector Jay By The Way, who kind of smells like cheese. I can't help but think of Kyler and how he smells so good all the time, never like rancid cheese. I wish he was the one with his arm around me, but no, he's probably back home, making out with my sister.

My mood nosedives and smacks against the ground like a squashed bug. *Yuck. Why the hell did I have to think that?*

Between the mental image my mind just conjured up and Jay By the Way's cheesy smell, I feel like I'm going to hurl. I want to slide out from under Jay's arm and get some fresh air, but I can't think of an excuse that won't make me look completely deranged, so he ends up keeping his arm there until we go through security. While Jay's emptying out his pockets, I bolt away from him for the stairs.

"Hey, Isa, wait up," Indigo says as she chases after me.

I pause at the bottom of the stairway and wait for her to catch up. When she reaches me, out of breath, I give her an *are you kidding me* look.

"What's that look for?" she asks innocently as she fans her face with her hand.

"Those guys were gross and smelled like bad cheese. Seriously, if that's your definition of excitement, then count me out."

"That's not even close to what I meant by excitement." She kicks off her shoes and tips her head up to take in all the stairs.

"We could take the elevator," I say, eyeballing her bare feet.

"No way. That's like cheating the excitement." She steps back with her heels in her hands then sprints forward, laughing as she charges up the first flight of stairs. "Race you to the top."

Laughing, I barrel after her and up the stairway. People skitter out of our way as we jog side-by-side up each flight of stairs. With each step, I feel closer to soaring, closer to flying away from reality, like I'm outrunning my problems.

By the time we arrive to the second floor, though, we slowed down to a sluggish walk, because, holy crap, there are a lot of stairs.

"My feet hurt," Indigo gripes, catching her breath. "But this makes it totally worth it."

"Holy shit, this is so cool." I slip my fingers through the railing and stare down at the glittering city stretched out below us."

"It's more than cool. It's exciting." Indigo reaches into her purse and fishes out her phone as I shut my eyes and breathe in the cool air kissing my cheeks.

While it might seem lame to most, tonight has been one of the best nights of my life. I've never ran around and had fun without worrying about being judged by my sister or scolded by my mom.

"I feel so . . . I don't know, free," I say as I open my eyes.

"That's how you should feel all of your life." She leans in close to me and snaps a picture of us with her camera phone. "Look how good you look," she says as she admires the picture. "And happy."

As I examine the photo, I think about all the family photos on the wall back home, most of which don't include me. But the few my mom let me be in, I never smiled, mostly because I felt uncomfortable, like I didn't belong.

"I do look happy, don't I?" I smile at the girl in the photo, a girl who only hours ago didn't exist. "Thanks, Indigo, for everything."

"Dude, we're only getting started." She puts the phone away then we turn back to the view. "By the time this trip is over, there's going to be so many pictures of you smiling you're going to be posting them for days."

I don't bother telling her that I don't have a social media account, that I don't have friends, so there's no point. Maybe when I get home, I'll change that, too. Maybe I'll change everything. And maybe that change will finally make Hannah see me differently.

The plan is far from perfect, but standing up on the Eiffel Tower, stories high from the ground, anything feels possible. I wish I could hold onto the moment forever. But then we have to leave, and with each step down the stairway, I feel the perfection fading as I head back down to reality.

Chapter
FIVE

By the time we make it back to the hotel room, my grandma is waiting for us, and she doesn't look very happy.

"Where the hell have you two been?" she asks as she stands up from the bed, swaying to the side, a little tipsy.

"Um," I glance at Indigo for help, "we were out walking."

Indigo slips her purse off and sets it on the table. "Chill, Grandma Stephy. We just went and did a little sightseeing."

She scowls at us. "You should have told me you were leaving. I was worried sick."

"We honestly thought you wouldn't even notice." Indigo flops down on the bed and yawns. "You've been super busy with your friends."

"Of course I noticed. I'm old, not blind." She inches toward me, and I can smell the alcohol rolling off her. "I promised your dad I wouldn't let you wander off."

"Really?" A smile starts to touch my lips. *My dad cares about me?*

But then Grandma Stephy hesitates, and I know she's lying.

"He really didn't say that, did he?" Sighing, I sink down in a chair to untie my boots.

"He might not have said it, but he'd kill me if anything happened to you," she says.

I keep my head down, focusing on unlacing the boots. "What were you and my dad talking about while you guys were in your bedroom?" I don't know why I ask. It just sort of slips out.

Indigo lets out a cough. "Not right now. She's too upset."

"What do you mean, 'Not right now. I'm too upset'?" Grandma Stephy asks, sounding drunkenly confused. When neither of us responds, she warns, "Okay, one of you two better start talking; otherwise, I'll ground your asses to the room for the rest of the trip."

"I'm nineteen," Indigo says, pushing up on her elbows. "You can't ground me."

"And I'm sixty and don't give a shit how old you are," Grandma Stephy snaps. "I'll ground you if I want to."

Indigo tenses and keeps her trap shut.

I want to back off, too, but now that I've opened Pandora's Box, there's no going back. All these words just keep pouring out of me. "Is my mom . . . Did my dad . . . Who's my real mom, Grandma Stephy?"

Her eyes widen, and I literally feel the perfection and freedom I felt on the Eiffel Tower go *poof.*

"I heard some of the stuff you and my dad said and . . . Lynn isn't my real mom, is she?" I ask, sounding eerily calm. "That's why she hates me so much."

Grandma Stephy's lips part, but then she rapidly shakes her head. "No, I'm not going to lie to you anymore. I told your father I was sick of this bullshit and that it was time to tell you. That they couldn't just keep treating you like crap—that it was time. And I meant it." She sits down in a chair beside me and squares her shoulders. "Isa, I love you to death. You need to understand that, okay? I love you so much and you're my fantastic, wonderfully weird, keep-me-on-my-toes granddaughter. Your grandpa loved you, too. He even told me once that you were his favorite."

"Hey," Indigo says, but then holds up her hands. "You know what. Never mind. I'm not going to open my mouth anymore tonight."

"Good girl," Grandma Stephy says to her, then focuses back on me. "I need to know you understand all of this. That you're loved."

I nod apprehensively, picking at my fingernails. "Okay, I get it."

"And your dad loves you, too," she tries to press.

"Okay." This time, I sound way less sure.

"I know he's not the best dad in the world, but I promise he loves you," she insists, looking a tad bit apprehensive. "He just hasn't always been able to show it."

"And what about Lynn?" I'm looking her dead in the eyes, so I see the fear flicker across her face.

She swallows hard. "Lynn is . . ." She rubs her hand across her face, looking stressed.

"She's not my mom," I answer for her in an uneven voice.

She looks utterly remorseful. "I'm so sorry, Isa. I really am. I don't want you to hurt, but I guess there's no easy way for you to learn about this."

Her words sink in, but it takes a moment or two for

them to really, *really* hit me. And fucking hell, they hurt, like a kick to the shin, a slam of the elbow, a gash to your heart hurt.

"Who's my real mom?" I ask quietly, refusing to look at Indigo, even though I can feel her trying to catch my gaze.

Grandma Stephy smashes her lips together as her eyes well up. "I wish I could tell you, but . . ." She kneels down in front of me. "I don't know who she is. Only your dad does . . . and Lynn. They've kept it a secret from the rest of the family, which was pretty easy for them, since they barely keep in contact with anyone except for the few reunions they attended."

Her arms circle around me, and she hugs me with everything she has in her. "The only reason I know about any of this is because your dad once asked me to raise you. Your mother . . . she couldn't take care of you for some reason, and your dad . . . well, at first he asked me if I could take care of you, because he didn't want to put you into foster care. But then something changed, and he decided he wanted to keep you. I tried to talk him out of it, especially because of Lynn, but he's too goddamn thickheaded to listen to anything I say." She leans back and takes my hands in hers.

I realize my fingers are shaking—that my entire body is shaking. "My dad never said why he took me in?" I whisper. "Why he changed his mind? Or why my mom needed to give me away?"

She shakes her head sadly. "I'm sorry, honey, but he never talks about it at all. The only time it's ever been brought up is over the phone the few weeks before they dropped you off with me, and that's because I forced the subject on him. I was tired of the way they treated you, and wanted to get some goddamn answers over what the hell happened fourteen years ago between your mother and him."

My mind swirls with confusion. "Wait . . . fourteen years . . ."

Her hold tightens on my hand, like she's afraid I'm going to run. "You lived with your mother for a few years before you went to go live with your dad."

I press my quivering lips together as tears burn in my eyes. "Why can't I remember any of this?"

"Honey, you were barely three when all this happened." Her voice is gentle, but her hold on my hand is firm as tears slide down my cheeks. "I know this is hard to take in, but—"

Before she can finish that thought, I yank my hands out of hers and run to the bathroom. "I think I'm going to be sick," I say, then slam the door shut and lock it.

After I throw up the wine I drank earlier, I sink to the tiled floor in front of my bag. I dig out my sketchpad and open it up to one of my favorite comics I drew, starring me and the woman I always wished was my mom. Maybe she wasn't just a wish, though. Maybe she was a faint memory I was trying to hold onto in dark times.

I touch the dark lines I meticulously drew. "Who are you?" I whisper.

Silence is my only answer, and it hurts almost as badly as my heart.

Curling up into a ball, I hug the sketchbook to my chest. Indigo wanted me to spend the summer discovering myself, but how the hell am I supposed to do that when I have no idea where I came from?

After bawling my eyes out for what feels like hours, I finally pull myself off the floor and drag my ass out of the bathroom. The lights are still on, but Indigo is passed out in one of the beds, still wearing her dress, snoring away.

My eyes are so swollen I can barely see anything, but I stand with confidence. I have to in order to hide the nerves sloshing around inside me. "When I get back, I want to find her," I tell Grandma Stephy.

She quickly aims the remote at the television, shuts off the show she was watching, and rubs the sleepiness from her eyes. "Honey, I'm not sure that's a good idea."

"I don't care if it's a good idea or not." I sit down on the edge of the bed, still holding onto my sketchbook. "It's what I want—need—to do. All my life, I felt like I was crazy, because I never, ever fit in with my family. And now I learn the reason why . . . and I want to know who she is, if she's like me. Maybe she can understand me." *Maybe she'll love me.*

Grandma Stephy ruffles her hair into place as she sits up in the bed and lowers her feet to the floor. "Isa, I know it's been hard living in that house, but I worry what'll happen to you if this doesn't turn out the way you want it to."

"But I don't even know how I want it to turn out," I point out. "I mostly just feel . . . lost right now."

She scoots toward me. "I hate to be blunt, but I feel like I have to." She blows out a deafening breath. "But there was a reason your mother chose to give you to your father. Whether it's because she couldn't take care of you, or . . ." She shakes her head. "I just want you to make sure you think about all the scenarios, how this could turn out before you dive into this."

I get where she's coming from. I can think of a ton of reasons off the top of my head of how this could end up going down. From my real mother being just as mean as Cruella de Lynn, to her being dead.

God, what if she is dead? What if I never get to know her? What if I continue to drift through life feeling so out of place?

I have to know. Have to understand. Where I came from. What makes me tick. What makes me so strange. What makes me . . . well, me. And even though I know it might hurt more than anything else, I have to know why she gave me up.

"If I do that—If I spend the next few months thinking about how this is going to turn out—and I still want to find her when I get back, will you help me?" I ask.

She's silent for a maddening amount of time, and I end up chanting one of my songs to keep from shouting at her.

Chocolate fudge. Caramel. Cinnamon rolls. I wonder if my mom bakes . . .

"If that's what you decide you want to do, then yes; I'll help you," she finally agrees, but she doesn't sound happy about it.

"Thank you, Grandma." I feel even more nervous for some reason, now knowing I could possibly find my real mom. What will I say to her when I see her? What will she say?

"Don't thank me yet." Grandma Stephy points to the other bed. "Now, get some sleep. I have a lot of fun things planned for us tomorrow."

I nod then climb into bed, still grasping onto the sketchbook. I may have told Grandma Stephy I'd really think this through, but I already know what my decision will end up being. Like Indigo said, good or bad, life is about experiences. And this is one experience I'm going through with, even if the outcome is brutal.

Chapter SIX

Paris turns out to be fun. Like a lot of a lot of fun. And we spend so much time sightseeing, tasting the food, and going shopping that I don't have too much time to dwell over my family situation. Still, during the late hours of the night, when Indigo is snoring and Grandma Stephy is tossing and turning, I lie awake in my bed going over every single memory I can scrounge up, trying to figure out how I missed it. Missed the truth. It's hard to take in, hard not to cry, and sometimes I let the tears soak my pillow. I just make sure that when the sun comes up, I'm bright-eyed, bushy-tailed, and ready to go on whatever adventure Indigo has planned for us.

"I'm so exhausted," Indigo says to Grandma Stephy as we get on the elevator to go up to our room. We've been in London for a few days now, and there are so many sights to see, like Big Ben and the Tower Bridge, that we've had hardly any time to rest. "I think I'm going to crash early tonight."

We've been on our trip for a couple of weeks now, so when she catches my eye and gives me *the look*, I know her feigned exhaustion is just a ruse. She really has a hidden agenda for us tonight. I'm excited to see what she has planned and cross my fingers that maybe it'll wear me out enough I'll pass out by the time we go to bed.

"That's okay. I was thinking about going out with some of my friends, anyway," Grandma says as the elevator doors glide open. She steps out into the hallway and we follow. "But could you two girls do me a favor?"

"Of course, Grandma Stephy, we'd be more than happy to." Indigo lays on her charm thickly.

"Make sure the door shuts all the way when you decide to sneak out." Grandma Stephy grins at us as she digs the keycard out of her purse. "Last time, you left it open. You were lucky we didn't get robbed."

Indigo gives her a guilty look. "That was all the way back in Paris. If you knew we were sneaking out all this time, then why didn't you say anything?"

Grandma Stephy swipes the keycard into the slot on our room door. "Because I didn't want to ruin the fun of sneaking out."

"But you freaked out the one time you found out we left the room," Indigo points out as the three of us enter the small, quaint room. "Why do you suddenly not care what we do?"

"I care. But I figured you two need to have some fun." She looks at me, and I know by that *you two* she really means *me*. Grandma Stephy sits down to take off her shoes. "But now that we've got that all out into the open, I'd prefer if you two told me where you were going and I didn't have to track you down with that little thing on your phone."

"What thing?" Indigo asks as she unzips her suitcase.

"That little tracker thing that lets you know where your phone is," Grandma Stephy gets up and heads into the bathroom to take a shower.

I flop down on the bed and stretch my arms and legs out. "So does it lessen our fun that she's known this whole time what we've been up to? Because that whole we're-being-so-rebellious-and-it-makes-this-so-much-more-fun speech you gave when we snuck out to go clubbing seems pretty insignificant now."

"Nah, we still had fun, didn't we?" she asks with her head tucked down as she rummages through her bag for the perfect outfit.

"That we did," I agree, sitting up. "So what're we doing tonight? Or is it another surprise?"

She looks up at me, grinning as she throws a shimmery black dress at my face. "Tonight, we're going to find you a guy."

I set the dress down on the bed and run my fingers along the glittery fabric, smoothing out the wrinkles. "I don't need to find a guy."

"Liar. You so need to find a guy, so you can get over that Kyler dude."

During a drunken conversation, I told Indigo about Kyler. She wasn't a huge fan of my crush on him, and said I deserved a guy who actually tried to spend time with me. I wanted to argue that we technically have spent time together, but knew my point was probably moot, since a few weekends doesn't really count.

Knowing there's no point in arguing with her, I get up and wiggle into the dress then curl my hair. I apply some dark red lipstick and kohl eyeliner then add a drop of eye glitter, just because I love looking sparkly sometimes. Since I'm a newbie at the hair and makeup thing, I make sure to get Indigo's approval.

"You look fantastic," she says, admiring my hand-iwork as she douses her hair in hairspray. "Seriously, you've caught onto this whole makeup and hair stuff way faster than I expected you to."

"Thanks." While I appreciate her approval, there are times where I still feel like the girl with shiny brown and green hair, wearing the glittery, probably too short dress isn't me. That I look ridiculous and everyone around me knows it.

My phone suddenly buzzes from the nightstand. Indigo and I trade a quizzical look, because the thing never goes off.

I hurry over and pick it up, worried there might be something wrong at home. But my confusion only deepens when I see the message is from Kai.

> *Kai: U haven't sent me any pics yet :(At first I thought maybe it's because u forgot all about your cute, sexy neighbor next door, but then I realized how impossible that could be and started worrying that maybe something bad happened to u. That's it, right? Something bad happened to u?*
>
> *Me: So you're saying u would rather something bad happen to me?*
>
> *Kai: Ha! I knew that'd get u to respond.*
>
> *Me: Whatever. I was never ignoring u, since this is the first time u sent me a message.*
>
> *Kai: I didn't want to seem too needy. But then I realized it wasn't about me. It was about your wellbeing.*

I roll my eyes. I can almost picture Kai smiling as he texts me, totally amused with himself.

Kai: So where's my pic?

"You should probably send him the one we took at the top of the Eiffel Tower. You looked amazing in it," Indigo says, reading the message from over my shoulder. "But first, you have to explain to me who Kai is."

"He's Kyler's young brother who loves to annoy me," I say, sinking down on the bed.

She coils a strand of her hair around her finger. "Annoy you, huh?" She seems wistful about something. "Because from what I read through the text, he seems like he's flirting with you."

I laugh so hard I almost pee myself. "Kai isn't flirting with me. Trust me. He's just made it his life mission to annoy the crap out of me." I start to send Kai the pic Indigo suggested, but then stop myself.

I don't fully understand why. Part of me whispers that my hesitancy is that I don't trust him. But the other part of me whispers that I'm just not ready to take these moments overseas—this fantasy world I've been living, where I feel like I can be anyone and do anything—and share it with my old life.

Me: Don't have any cool pics yet. Sorry.

I leave it at that and put my phone away. He doesn't reply. I don't know why I'm surprised or a tiny bit disappointed, but I am. The sucky part is I don't know what I'm more disappointed about—Kai's silence, or the fact I was too afraid to send him a damn photo.

I shake the feeling off, though, and focus on tonight. I focus on my next life experience, because that's what I should be doing.

Chapter
SEVEN

Four hours later, Indigo and I get in line to ride the London Eye, a ginormous Ferris wheel with oval passenger pods that are covered in windows that are supposed to give you a great view of the city. Indigo and I met Peter just before we got in line to get on, and Peter just happened to bring along his friend, Nyle. Although, I don't think it was by accident. This is a setup. I get that. What I don't get is what I'm supposed to do with this cute British guy who keeps looking at me like I'm adorable.

"You want me to get us a drink or something before we get on?" Nyle asks, seeming almost as nervous as I am.

I try to smile like Indigo does all the time, whenever she's flirting. "Sure. That sounds great."

He smiles before stepping out of the line to head over to the concession stand.

Indigo gives me this knowing look and I have no idea how to react. Just what exactly does she think is going to happen on this fun-filled Ferris wheel ride of ours?

I shake my head at her then take in the sights around me, the bright lights, the soft music from the street performs, and the energized buzz in the air.

"It's a beautiful night, isn't it?" Nyle asks when he returns to the line.

I tear my attention off the starry sky and catch him checking me out. He smiles sheepishly at me as he hands me a bottle of Coke.

"Yeah, it's really pretty here." I twist the cap off the bottle and glug down a few swallows, giving myself some time to figure out what to say to him.

It's not that I'm shy, but I don't feel as comfortable around him as I do with people I know.

We spend the next ten minutes in awkward silence before we make it to the front of the line and get onto the Ferris wheel. While Indigo chats with Peter about New York, Nyle gets a nervous energy boost and starts babbling to me about himself. I try to listen. I really do. But his opening liner is that he's a math major, and I end up zoning in and out of the conversation, more fascinated with the breathtaking view than the guy next to me.

I feel like an asshole. I mean, Nyle is trying to get to know me, telling me about his classes, his love for numbers, canoeing, and water polo. I nod my head every so often and offer him a few smiles. He has to be getting exhausted of me and my silence; at least, that's what I figure when he suddenly grows quiet. But when I look at him, he's leaning in for a kiss.

"You're really beautiful, you know that?" he whispers, his gaze flicking back and forth between my eyes and my lips. "And a really good listener."

So I've been told, I think as his lips inch toward mine.

I hesitate, deciding. Just kiss him, even though I have

no interest in him? The idea seems both appealing and appalling. I mean, on the one hand, he's super cute, if you like that preppy, slacks-and-sweater sort of look. On the other hand, I've been bored to death the entire last couple of hours.

"Hey, Isa, come chat with me for a sec, would you?" Indigo interrupts the moment, grabbing me by the arm and towing me to the opposite side of the pod, away from listening ears. "What are you doing?" she whispers, glancing back at Peter and Nyle.

"Um, hanging out," I reply, super confused by the astounded look on her face.

"No, I mean with Nyle," she hisses, unzipping her purse. "It looked like you were about to faint when he leaned in to kiss you."

I scrunch up my nose. "You were watching that?"

"Don't pretend like I'm some pervert. I was just keeping an eye on you, like I promised you I would." She pulls out a tube of lipstick and applies a coat to her lips. "Now, do you want to tell me why you looked sickened over the fact that a hot guy wants to kiss you?"

"I'm not sickened by the fact." I flick a glance in Nyle's direction and he smiles at me. "I don't know if I should be kissing him, when we have nothing in common."

She drops her lipstick back into her purse. "Oh, Isa." She ruffles my hair with her hand, something she does whenever she thinks I'm being naïve. "You have so much to learn."

"About what exactly?" I comb my fingers through my hair, smoothing the strands back into place. "Kissing complete strangers?"

"About kissing in general." She zips up her purse and rubs her lips together. "Look, if you really don't want to kiss Nyle, then don't. But if you want to kiss him, but you're not, because you think kissing should be this fairy-tale experience of love at first sight, then I recommend you get over it and give kissing a try."

"But we have nothing in common, and honestly, I'm kind of bored."

"Okay, well, maybe kissing him will make things less boring."

"And what if it doesn't?"

She stares out the glass, the light from the city reflecting in her eyes. "If you kiss him and it sucks, then pretend to sneeze and I'll come rescue you."

"You want me to sneeze in his face?" I struggle not to laugh at the mental image of me sneezing in Nyle's face.

"It's the best way to get him to stop. But I think you should give the kissing thing a try." She swings around a couple making out near the center of the pod and heads back across toward the guys. "And hey, maybe this will help you get over the Kyler thing."

As I make my way back to Nyle, I can't help but think that maybe Indigo's right. Perhaps I should get over Kyler. After all, he's probably back home, in a lip lock with Hannah.

I wince as I realize how big of a possibility that is, and before I even know what I'm doing, I march straight up to Nyle and seal my lips with his.

He taste like beer, is the first thought that crosses my mind, which only makes me giggle.

Bravo, Isa, on being the weirdest kisser in the world.

Nyle seems to find me amusing, though, and chuckles along with me, before deepening the kiss. While there's no fireworks or explosions, I do discover that kissing is fun. I might have to try it again sometime.

Or a lot.

We kiss a lot that night, in the pod, on the street in

front of Big Ben, and at a bakery shop we stop at to get cupcakes.

At the end of the night, Nyle and I say goodbye. We don't exchange numbers or emails. We just kiss and tell each other we had fun. There's no expectations to try to talk to each other again and I like that.

"Was I right? Or was I right?" Indigo asks me.

It's well after midnight, but I feel wide awake as we skip through the glitzy hotel lobby and toward the elevators.

"You were right." I push the up button and wait for the doors to open.

Indigo is grinning like a dork as we jump into the elevator, but her mood swiftly shifts. "You are having fun, though, right? I just want to make sure that you are. I know after what you found out in Paris . . ." She sighs, slipping off her purple platform shoes. "I just want to make sure you're having fun, despite what you found out."

"I promise I am." I link arms with her. "You've done good, cuz."

"Why thank you, cuz." She laughs, slumping back against the wall. "So what did you think of your first kiss?"

"It actually wasn't that bad. And Nyle seems like a great kisser."

"Did it help you forget about Kyler?"

"It actually did for a while," I answer truthfully.

"Good. I'm glad." She presses our floor button with her toe, too lazy to lean forward and do it with her fingers. "You should have seen the look on Nyle's face when you kissed him. He was so into it."

I replay the kiss in my head. The girl in the memory looks like me, yet she's almost unrecognizable, doing things I never thought I'd do.

I look at my reflection in the mirror on the wall. My eyes are big, my cheeks flushed, and my lips are swollen. I look wired, happy, hyped up on life and experiences. I wonder if Kyler, Hannah, or even Kai saw me right now, they'd know who I was. I think about texting Kai a photo of me and finding out, but am too worried he'll know exactly who I am, still see me as the nerdy girl next door. And I'm too worried he won't, that through this exterior transformation, I've somehow lost my entire identity.

But that can't be true. I still feel the same. For the most part, anyway.

I vow to myself right there and then that I won't lose sight of who I am, no matter what happens. Not just while I'm here, but when I get back home too.

Chapter
EIGHT

Over the next couple of weeks or so, I hold onto my promise to myself as much as I can. It becomes increasingly complicated, though, with each crazy endeavor Indigo and I embark on.

Like the first time we went clubbing in Scotland. We spend half the night chatting with complete strangers before we head into a club. Indigo orders us drinks then fixes her attention into coaxing me into dancing with her.

"You want me to what?" I gape at her like she's a raving lunatic.

She laughs as she picks up a shot glass. "I said let's dance. We look too hot not to dance."

While I agree that we both look hot in our short dresses with our hair all done, I don't think dancing is necessary, especially when I can't dance.

"Don't look at me like that. You'll be fine." She angles back her head, throws down the shot, and then sets the glass down on the counter.

"Yeah, clearly you've never seen me dance; otherwise, you wouldn't be suggesting that," I say, peering around at the people laughing, drinking, and grinding all up on each other.

"That's a lame excuse," she says. "Give me a better one and I'll let you off the hook."

The dim lighting makes it hard to see anyone's face, and with the atmosphere buzzing and the music throbbing, there isn't a good excuse I can see anywhere.

I look back at her, sulking. "Do I have to?"

"You don't have to do anything," she says, shimmying her hips as she backed toward the dance floor. "But you're missing out on one of life's great experiences." Then she raises her hands in the air as she reaches the edge of the dance floor, rocking out to a bass driven song. "Dance like no one's watching!" she shouts over the music then starts head banging like a freakin' punk rock chick.

I wait for someone to laugh at her, but I quickly realize no one gives a shit about what anyone else is doing. Everyone's too focused on their own thing, like I should be.

So, with a deep breath, I gag down my shot and amble for the dance floor.

It takes me a few minutes to warm up and let loose, but I get there. There's something invigorating about dancing, like there's no tomorrow. With every laugh, sway of my hips, flail of my arms, I feel more like a different person. Riskier. More daring. Someone who lives life, instead of just existing in it.

So I keep dancing.

I dance until my feet hurt.

Until they blister.

Until I'm so damn tired I can't think.

By the time Indigo and I make it back to the hotel, I'm dripping with sweat, tired as hell, but have a huge-ass smile on my face, totally high on life.

"You look so happy," Indigo remarks as we lazily wander down the hallway toward our room.

"I am happy. Like really, really happy," I say as she rests her head on my shoulder and leans all her weight against me.

I do the same thing back to her and we giggle.

"I'm too tired. Hold me up," she whines through our giggling.

"No way. You hold me up. You're the one who made me dance."

"Well, you're the one who refused to stop."

Right as we're about to tip over, my phone vibrates from inside my pocket. I don't have to look to know who the message is from, because he's the only person who's texted me during this entire trip.

> *Kai: I'm still waiting on that photo. And don't say u don't have any good ones again, because I'm not buying it. You've been gone for over two months and there's no way u haven't taken any good photos yet.*

> *Me: What's up with the pressure? It's starting to stress me out.*

> *Kai: You're stressed out??? Think about how stressed I've been. I mean, I haven't heard anything from u except for a few messages here and there, and for all I know, this might not even be u. Maybe some British dude stole your phone and is texting me, pretending to be u.*

> *Me: Wow, that's quite the story u came up with.*

Kai. Thanks. I'm pretty proud of it myself.

Me: Well, sorry to burst your awesome story bubble, but I'm not a British dude. I'm just plain old Isa.

Kai: Prove it. Send me the most awesome pic you've taken so far. That's the only way I'll believe u.

"I think he just wants to have a picture of you," Indigo mutters as she reads the messages from over my shoulder.

"Doubtful."

Me: Can't right now. Sorry.

Kai: I'm seriously disappointed. I was holding onto the hope that you'd finally send me one so I could be entertained at this lame-ass party.

Me: First of all, why on earth would a photo of me entertain u? And second, if you're at a party, why r u bored? Isn't that why people go to parties? So they can be unbored?

Kai: Unbored? Hmmm . . . I'm not sure what that means.

Me: Hey, don't mock my awesome made up words. I work hard on them.

Kai: I actually remember that about u. U always tried to convince me that things could be unglittery and unzombie-like. I thought it was funny.

Me: That's because I'm a funny girl. Duh. I thought u knew that already.

Kai: I did . . . Still do. Now please, send me something fun to look at so I can be unbored.

Me: Only if u say pretty please.

Indigo giggles. "Holy shit, Isa, you're totally flirting with him."

My cheeks flush. "I am not."

"You so are."

"So am not . . . I'm just a little tipsy."

"So? You were a little tipsy toward the end of that night we hung out with Nyle and Peter, and I didn't see you flirting with them." She gives me an accusing look.

My cheeks blaze with heat as I put the phone away without sending Kai another message. "Well, I know Kai."

She examines my face intently and I wonder what the hell she sees. "You should ask him for a pic, so I can see what he looks like."

I shake my head. "No way. Then you'd try to push me to flirt with him even more."

"Why? Is he hot?"

I shrug. "Sure. I mean, a lot of girls at my school think so."

"Do you think so?" she presses.

I sigh. "Yeah, but so what? It's not like he'd ever think the same way about me."

Indigo targets me with a *don't be silly, Isa* look, something she does a lot. "No guy is that obsessed with getting a picture from a girl unless he likes her."

"Kai doesn't like me." I grit my teeth, thinking about how embarrassed he looked when we were spotted walking home together. "Trust me."

"It seems like he does to me. I think you might just be in denial, because you don't think there's any way a guy could ever like you."

"I don't think that anymore." I glance down at my

red and black dress and my long, hairless legs. "But Kai hasn't seen me like this. He only knows the awkward, hairy-legged beast Isa."

"Just because you shaved your legs and do your hair doesn't make you a different person," she says as we near our room. "You're still the same Isa that came on this trip. You just have a little more confidence now."

"Okay, so that might be true, but Kai still doesn't like me." When she gives me a doubtful look, I give her a brief recap of mine and Kai's history.

"Maybe he feels bad about blowing you off now. People do change a lot from when they were thirteen," she says after I'm finished. She uses the keycard to open the room door, but pauses before she walks in. "And it does kind of sound like he's been trying to be friends with you over the last year or so."

I start to protest, but my jaw snaps shut as I hear the sound of moaning coming from inside our room. Indigo's eyes pop wide as the mattress squeaks and we hear Grandma Stephy groan, "Oh, Harry."

"Oh. My. God." Indigo rapidly shuts the door and we both sprint off toward the elevators.

Only when the elevators slide shut, does Indigo finally speak again.

"I don't know what's worse . . ." She punches the main floor button. " . . . what we just heard, or the fact Grandma Stephy is getting more action on this trip than either of us."

Laughter bursts from my lips, and Indigo quickly joins in. It's the silliest moment ever, but I'll cherish it forever. It's because of moments like these that I've made it through this trip without sinking into a pit of despair over what I learned about my mother. Yeah, I know that soon I'll be back home and I'll have to finally deal with the truth. But I'll always have these memories, even if some of these moments are really awkward. Through the good, bad, and painfully embarrassing, this trip changed me. Made me stronger. More confident. And hopefully that'll help me when I get home.

I'm laughing so hard by the time we arrive on the main floor that my ribs actually hurt. "So what do we do now?" I ask as I stumble out into the vacant lobby.

Indigo's gaze skims the front desk, which the receptionist has abandoned, then her eyes land on the pool sign just to our right.

"I have an idea," she says, dragging me toward the doors with a wicked glint in her eyes.

"But I don't have my swimsuit," I protest, digging my heels into the floor. "And it's after hours."

"So what?" She swipes the keycard through the slot then tugs open the door. "There's no one here to stop us, is there?"

She's right. There's not a single person around. But why would there be, when it's four o'clock in the morning?

The door bangs shut behind us as we step into the faintly lit room that smells like chlorine. The pool gently ripples in front of us, begging to be dipped in.

"What about swimsuits?" I tentatively inch up to the edge, slip off my heels, and dip my toe into the lukewarm water.

"Swimsuits are for amateurs." She shimmies out of her dress and kicks it off to the side. "Besides, you can't cross skinny-dipping off your list if you're wearing a swimsuit."

"Skinny-dipping isn't on my list," I say as she cannonballs into the water, wearing nothing but her underwear and bra.

"The water feels so nice," she remarks as she floats on top of the water, her hair spread out like a veil.

She looks so relaxed and the water so inviting.

"Oh, what the hell?" I peel off my dress and wade into the water.

She's right. The water does feel fantastic. And while the moment is relaxing and not as heart-pumping as dancing in a club or kissing guys on Ferris wheels, it's one I'm glad I lived.

An hour later, we climb out of the pool, dry off, and slip into our dresses. We don't go back into the room, instead, heading out to the park across the street, where we watch the sunrise.

"I can't believe we have to go home in a few weeks," Indigo says as we rest against each other on a bench near a section of trees.

"I know, but at least we got to experience it, right?" I squint as the sun peeks through the morning haze and lights up the sky.

"I've taught you very, very well, young grasshopper. I feel like such a proud mama right now." She pats my head and we both giggle.

Then we settle against each other and simply watch the sky. I feel so at peace right now with myself, yet afraid at the same time that I won't have this feeling ever again. Suddenly, I find myself digging out my phone and snapping a photo of me with wet hair and slightly smeared makeup, the sunrise as my background. I have a content smile on my face and actually look fairly decent.

This was who I was once, I type then hit send.

I have no idea why I chose those words, other than I'm still a little high on such an amazing night. A minute later, I instantly regret it, but now there's no going back.

I spend the rest of the morning with Indigo, waiting

for Kai to reply.

He never does.

I'm not sure how I feel about it. Thankfully, I don't have too much time to wallow over it, because hours later, Indigo and I are moving on to our next adventure.

Chapter
NINE

"Oh. My. God," Indigo groans as she stuffs her face with a double cheeseburger. "I missed you, my dear, sweet hamburger, even though you treat me poorly and go straight to my thighs."

I giggle in the backseat of Grandma Stephy's car then pop a fry into my mouth. "The food wasn't that bad over there," I say.

She narrows her eyes at me with a drizzle of grease dripping down her chin. "Dude, are you fucking crazy? It was terrible. Everything was either burnt or topped with some weird sauce." She sets the burger down on her lap and dunks a fry into a cup of ranch. "Good God, I've missed ranch on my fries. I'm seriously about to have a foodgasm."

"No foodgasms in the car," Grandma Stephy says as she turns the car off the main road.

I set the fry that I was about to eat down as I sudden-ly lose my appetite as we get closer to my house. We've been back in Sunnyvale for a couple of nights now, but this will be the first time I've been home in three months. And it'll be the first time I've seen my family since I discovered the secret about my mother.

It's crazy that I managed to hardly think about it the entire trip. Now that I'm back in the states, it's all I can think about twenty-four seven.

Time to get some answers.

"Are you sure you don't want to stay with me for a little bit longer?" Grandma Stephy asks me for the millionth time.

"I wish I could," I say truthfully. "But my senior year starts in a couple of days, and I need to get stuff ready."

"What stuff?" Indigo stares at me while she chews on a huge mouthful of hamburger. "We already have your wardrobe fully taken care of. You're seriously going to look edgy hot."

I smile. She's been calling my style edgy hot ever since around London, when I started wearing boots and leather jackets with dresses and knee-high socks. "I'm not talking about needing to get clothes. I'm talking about getting supplies and stuff. You know, pencils and notebooks and books. I also need to get started on my blog again. I haven't done anything with it all summer, and I want to get it going again." I tuck a few strands of my long brown hair with reddish highlights behind my ear. "I actually think I'm going to blog about our trip."

"Good. It was an awesome trip full of tell-all adventures." She grins at me, and I smile back. "Although, not all of them are tell-all." She points a finger at me, warning me to keep my mouth shut about some of the more interesting stuff we did on our little trip, like our skinny-dipping adventure in the pool.

I draw my fingers over my lips, silently telling her I'll

keep my trap shut.

"What are you two girls yammering about?" Grandma Stephy asks as she makes a right into my neighborhood.

"Nothing," Indigo and I say at the same time.

Grandma Stephy shakes her head. "Fine. Keep your secrets. Just know that I have mine, too."

"Oh, we know you do," Indigo says then moans through a giggle, "Oh, Harry."

Grandma Stephy's eyes widen. "What the hell are you talking about?"

"You don't know?" Indigo questions with doubt.

Grandma Stephy rolls her eyes. "How on Earth would I know what the hell you're giggling about? You two think everything's funny."

"Only things that are funny," Indigo says through choked laughter. "I know this might be past your time, but the customary rule for having roommates is to leave a tie on the door when you're hooking up. That way, someone doesn't accidentally walk in on something they don't want to see.

The two of them start bantering, and I sit back in the seat and watch the homes as we pass them.

I've never been a fan of where I live, but after traveling and seeing so many historical places, Gothic buildings, and even an underground tunnel filled with bones, I kind of hate the homes built to show off the upper class. But the hatred I feel for the houses dissipates the moment we pull up to my two-story home, and is replaced by the deepest, nerve-striking anger I've ever felt.

It's going to be okay. Everything is going to change. You're stronger now, and you're going to find out about your mother. Maybe you'll even be able to go live with her.

After my grandma parks the car, I get out, go around to the trunk, and start piling my bags onto the ground.

"Here, let me help you." Grandma Stephy shoos me out of the way, takes the last of my bags out, and sets them aside in the driveway. "You want me to help you carry them in?"

I shake my head. "I can do it."

"Are you sure?" she asks, stealing a hesitant glance toward my house, probably afraid to leave me.

"I'm positive," I say. "Would you stop worrying so much? Everything's going to be fine."

"You're my granddaughter. It's my job to worry about you." She pulls me in for a hug. "If you need anything at all, you call me, you hear?"

"You're still going to help me, right?" I ask. "You promised you would."

"I told you I'd look into it, and I will, but I really think the best thing to do is talk to your father." She pats my back. "Take a few days and let the trip wear off then call me, and we'll figure something out."

I nod, hugging her one last time before stepping away. "Thank you. Not just for the trip, but for everything."

"I just want you to be happy, Isa." She rounds the car and opens the driver's side door, calling out, "And remember, I'm only a thirty minute drive away."

"Aye, aye, Captain," I holler back.

Laughing, she gets inside the car.

I'm about to start up the driveway when the passenger window rolls down and Indigo sticks her head out.

"You know, I'm going to be visiting at least once a week to make sure you don't go back to your baggy clothes, caterpillar eyebrows, and furry beast legs look," she warns. "And if you're not living up to your full potential, you're in deep shit. I'm talking hours and hours of reading beauty magazines."

My face twists in disgust and I give her a salute. "Yes,

boss."

"And don't you ever forget that." She leans out to hug me. "I can also take care of your sister if you need me to. Seriously. I'm an expert in taking bitchy girls down from their pedestals."

I smile to myself, thinking about how mafia her words sound, kind of like the last thing Kai said to me.

Kai.

I scrunch up my nose. He never did text me back after I sent that photo. I'm not sure why, but it really started to bother me. Not in an oh-my-God-it's-the-end-of-the-world sort of way, but more in a why-did-he-bug-me-for-a-photo-if-he-was-just-going-to-dis-me way.

My gaze drifts to the house next door and then to my own oversized home. It's weird being back, so close to Kyler, Hannah, and Kai, when I no longer look like Swamp Thing. But changing my looks wasn't about any of them. I just felt an overwhelming need to change into a person who is more confident, and didn't base her looks on the negative comments her mother gave her over the years.

After Grandma Stephy and Indigo pull out onto the street, I hike up the driveway, towing two of my four bags with me.

I can do this. I'm Super Confident Girl, who fears no evil, who skinny-dips in the hotel pool late at night, and who dances at overcrowded clubs and kisses guys on Ferris wheels.

By the time I reach the backdoor, though, Super Confident Girl has turned into Freak the Fuck Out Girl. I let go of the bags and stare at the door.

"You can do this, Isa. Just walk on in and tell them to go . . ." I bite down on my lip as fear pulsates through me.

"Tell them to go what?" Kai's amused voice sails over my shoulder.

I sigh. Great. Just what I need right now. Intense, jokester guy next door who never texted me back.

"I was going to say *go fuck themselves*," I answer, turning around to face him.

He's rocking his typical look—a pair of shorts with no shirt. His blond hair's a hot mess, and an amused grin is playing at his lips. But the smile vanishes as he presses his lips together. His gaze skims across the boots, black floral dress, and leather jacket I'm wearing, lingering uncomfortably long on my bare legs. When his eyes land on my face, I feel like that poser again, the one who stepped out onto the streets of Paris wearing that red dress. The feeling has faded over the last few months, but it was easier to be confident with who I am now when I was in a club full of strangers who didn't know about my let-my-clothes-swallow-me-up-and-fade-me-into-the-background-of-my-sister's-shadow phase.

"You look . . ." A somewhat perplexed, somewhat intrigued look crosses his face, and I seriously get a little excited over what's about to come out of his mouth. "Weird."

"Oh, for the love of God." I turn back to my suitcases. Seriously. *Seriously?* All that changing and shaving and tweezing, and I get *weird* again.

"Hey, I didn't mean that in a bad way," he says, but I can hear him chuckling. "Seriously, Isa. I'm sorry."

I hear a thump and then the sound of footsteps heading my way. I spin back around then stumble back when I realize Kai is way up in my personal space.

"It sounded a lot better in my head," he says to me as I regain my footing. "But hearing it aloud . . . yeah, I'm thinking weird might not be a compliment."

"It's fine." I brush him off. "But, just for future reference, maybe you should repeat your compliments in your head a few times before saying them aloud."

"Duly noted." He smiles again, going right back to his goofy, jokester self. "You know, that photo you sent me didn't do you any justice. I mean, I could tell you looked different, but not this different."

I consider asking him why he never texted me back, but don't want to give him an opportunity to crack a joke about me obsessing over him.

"So, was the trip everything you hoped it would be and more?" he asks lightly.

I get whiplash from his sudden shift to formality, but whatever. "Yeah, it was pretty great. I seriously wish I could've stayed longer." Forever maybe.

"Where did you even go? You said overseas, but that could be a ton of places."

"That's because we went a ton of places." A smile touches my lips as I remember all the places I saw, all the people I met, how great I felt while on that trip. "But my favorite was probably Scotland."

He goes all bug-eyed. "Holy shit, you went to *Scotland?* I thought when you said you were going with your grandma that you'd go somewhere cliché like Paris."

"I did go to Paris too, with my grandmother *and* my cousin, Indigo, along with an entire old folks home," I say, shooting him a smile when he raises his brows like *what the hell?* "And FYI, Paris is awesome, and so are old people."

"Maybe it was just you that made the trip and Paris cool," he teases with a cocky grin.

I stick my finger into my mouth and pretend to gag. "That line was sooo cheesy."

"So what? Admit it. You missed my cheesiness."

"Never."

"Not at all?" He fakes a pout. "Wow, way to crush

my ego."

I want to tell him no, but can't bring myself to do so. Deep down, I might have missed it just a bit. "Your ego needs crushing."

He beams. "I knew you missed me."

I roll my eyes. "Cocky much?"

"I'm cocky all the time." He pauses, studying me in a way that makes me squirm. "You know, I don't think I believe you that Paris was awesome. I think I need proof." He makes grabby hands. "Let me see some pics so I can decide for myself."

"I already sent you one," I remind him. "You didn't seem that thrilled about it."

"I was too thrilled," he says. "You looked so content in that photo. It made me want to be there with you. I even made it my screensaver."

I resist another eye roll. "You so did not."

"I did too." He traces an x across his heart with his finger. "But I lost my phone, so I need new one."

"Are you being seriously? Because sometimes I can't tell."

"You think I'd lie to you?" he questions, jutting out his lip. When I stare at him, unimpressed, he sighs. "Look, I promise I'm not lying. I was at a party when you sent me the photo. I looked at it and remember thinking how great of a photo it was. Totally screensaver worthy. So that's what I did with it. Then I went back to the party, totally planning on texting you back and telling you how awesome of a photo is was. But then I got drunk and lost my phone." He shrugs. "Sorry. I really did like the photo."

He seems like he's being genuine, but considering our past, trusting Kai is complicated. I attempt to get a read on him, but he's doing that smoldering stare thing that makes him hard to read.

"Are you being serious right now about wanting to see all of my photos?" I ask. "Or is this like the time you asked to see my sketches then when I showed them to you, you told me you were just kidding and looked at me like I was a spazz."

"I never said I was joking around, and I don't think you're a spazz," he says, sounding appalled. "I said I was just teasing you."

"There's a difference?" I ask flatly.

He shakes his head, his lips twitching. "Isa, there's a huge-ass difference between joking around with someone and teasing them."

"Yeah, teasing's way, way worse."

"No, it isn't," he insists. "Teasing is a compliment. It means I like you enough to tease you."

"Well, if that's the case, then you must like me a freaking ton. Because you pretty much use all of your teasing energy on me. With everyone else, it's all," I flutter my eyelashes, "look into my eyes and swoon."

"First of all," he aims a finger at me, fighting back a laugh, "I never flutter my eyelashes."

"You might not think you do, but I've totally seen you do it before." I feel oddly gratified that I'm finally getting the upper hand in our conversation. Usually, he always gets me so flustered that I give up. But this time, he's the one getting all squirrely.

"Name one time," he says, his eyes burning with fierce determination.

"How about at Hannah's seventeenth birthday party?" I cross my arms and smirk as he grows fidgety. "You were trying to get her attention while she was swimming and you knelt down on the side of the pool, leaned in, and did this," I bat my eyelashes, "while whispering something to her. God knows what the hell you said, but it made her giggle, and you acted like a cocky asshole for the rest of the day."

His lip twitches, but more out of annoyance. "That was a long time ago, and I was really, really bored that day and trying to piss Kyler off, because I thought he had a thing for Hannah. But I'm not that guy anymore."

I choose to be completely ignorant over what he said about thinking Kyler had a thing for Hannah, and let Indigo's words about Kai replay in my mind. *Maybe he feels bad about blowing you off. People do change a lot from when they were thirteen.*

"Are you saying you don't flirt with Hannah anymore?" I ask. "Or you don't flutter your eyelashes anymore?"

"Both," he says, sticking out his hands again. "Now, let me see the photos of your trip."

Sighing, I retrieve my phone from my purse and search for the folder labeled *Trip*. "My cousin actually took most of the photos. She's into photography, but I did take some." I tap the folder to open it then hand him the phone. "They're not great or anything, but there's some decent ones."

After getting situated on the bottom step of the porch, he starts skimming through the photos, but stops on one of me standing with Indigo in front of a wall of skulls that form a heart. "Where's this?"

"That's the catacombs," I answer, sinking down on the stair beside him. "Which are all these tunnels that go under Paris."

He nods, browsing through a couple more photos then stops again. "Who's this guy feeding you a cupcake?"

"That's Nyle. He lives in London, and he's friends with this guy, Peter, who my cousin knew from here."

It was right after I kissed him. We'd gotten off the London Eye and stopped at a bakery. The photo was to be silly, but it still makes me smile as I look at it.

Kai doesn't say anything else as he finishes looking through the photos. Then he hands me back my phone, rests back on his elbows, and stretches out his long legs. "Okay, so I didn't want to ask, because I thought it'd be rude. But I can't stop thinking about it, so I'm going to ask; otherwise, I'm going to either lose my mind or my head's going to explode. But before I ask, I just want you to know that I'm not trying to be rude. I'm just curious," he says then stops talking. Just like that. After that long-ass speech.

"Dude, are you going to ask, or did you just say all that to drive me crazy?" I ask, stuffing my phone into my pocket.

His eyes sparkle mischievously. "I was just trying to show you how I was feeling. Do you feel like you're losing your mind yet from not having the answer?"

I pinch his side. I don't even know why I do it. Okay, maybe that's a lie. I've seen Indigo use the move on a couple of guys she was flirting with.

Holy shit! I'm flirting with Kai.

What the fuck is wrong with me?

"Wow, you're violent." Kai chuckles, rubbing his side where I pinched him.

"Sorry, I'm just impatient." I clasp my hands in front of me. "Would you please, please ask your question before I either lose my mind or my head explodes?"

"Fine, I'll tell you." He mockingly rolls his eyes. "Geez, Isa, there's no need to get overdramatic." He flashes me a playful grin when I glare at him, pretending to be more annoyed than I am. "So, what's up with the new look?"

"That's your question. Really?" I frown disappointedly. "I have to say, after all that build up, I thought you'd ask me something way more intense and awkward."

His brow cocks. "Like what? If you're a virgin or something?"

My cheeks flush, and I hate that he can see it. "No, that's not what I was thinking at all."

He grazes his finger across my cheek. "I forgot how cute you are when you blush."

The movement is so quick I barely register it, but my heart accelerates, my pulse pounding against my wrist, my neck . . . everywhere.

My body is a damn betrayer, though, and my mind is yelling at me to be pissed off at him. He's talking about the past, back when we used to hang out, and he has no right to talk about those moments he decided to pretend never happened.

"You've never seen me blush before," I lie, my voice a little shaky. I run my fingers over my hair, smoothing it into place. "And I decided to change my look. It's not a big deal."

"There has to be a reason behind it, especially since I know you hate dresses and makeup and all that girly shit."

"I've never hated girly shit. I was just confused . . . back then." *Back when you stabbed me in the heart.* "And I'm not that girly." I lift my feet and tap my boots together. "See. Totally not girly shoes."

He bites back a smile. "Still, you're way different, and usually there's a reason why someone does a complete flip of the switch."

I arch my brows. "You mean, like you?"

He grimaces. "Yeah, I guess so."

I consider his question, but the idea of telling him

what I discovered about myself and my family while I was on the trip terrifies me. "I'll show you mine if you show me yours."

His lips quirk, and his eyes darken. "What exactly are you talking about, Isa? Because when you say shit like that to me, my mind automatically goes right to the gutter." His gaze sweeps up and down my body, causing me to shiver. "But I'm more than happy to show you mine."

I roll my eyes and shove him, but laugh. "Don't be gross."

"Hey, you're the one who said it," he says with a grin.

"I meant I'll tell you why I changed if you tell me why you changed."

He considers what I said, but not for very long. "All right, keep your secrets then."

"Okay, I will." I'm only a tiny bit sad he didn't tell me, because I'm curious why he decided to go from jock to this laid-back, I-don't-give-a-shit-about-anything version of Kai. But mainly, I'm glad, because I don't want to tell him my secret.

He juts out his lip, pouting again. "You're really not going to tell me?"

"You know that doesn't work on me, right?" I push to my feet, brushing the dirt off the backs of my legs. "I gave you a chance to know, but you didn't want to take it."

He rises to his feet and stretches out his arms.

I try not to stare as his shorts ride lower, but I stare a little. Unlike Kyler, Kai isn't muscly. Toned, yes. Lean, absolutely.

"Well, maybe I'll change my mind," Kai says, crossing his arms over his chest and stealing my view from me. "Maybe I'll decide to tell you all my secrets, and then you'll have to tell me yours."

"When that happens, then that happens." I give a

nonchalant shrug.

"Okay, well . . ." He struggles for words, seeming a little unsure of my blasé attitude.

I smile, like a full on, evil villain, I-just-kicked-your-ass smile. He's so used to getting his way, and I can tell it's driving him crazy that I'm not caving to his charming smiles and adorable pouts.

"Smile all you want. Just know that I have tricks up my sleeve. I'll get you to tell me when you least expect it."

I raise my hands in front of me and dramatically gasp. "Oh no. Whatever should I do? Kai Meyers has got tricks up his sleeve and he's going to use them on me." I lower my hands as he glares at me. "You forget I know the side of you that had magic tricks up his sleeve and dreamt of being a magician."

"You promised you'd never say anything about that," he warns, aiming a finger at me. "And that was, like, when I was twelve. I outgrew that fucking weird phase."

"For your information, I liked that phase," I say, reaching for my suitcases. "You may think it's weird be-cause it's different, but different is so much better than normal." When he gives me a confusedly intrigued look, I ask, "Why are you looking at me like that?"

He shrugs, scuffing his boots against the concrete. "It's nothing."

"It's something." I tug on the bags and start dragging them up the stairs. "You're looking at me like I'm . . . I don't know, funny or something. And I wasn't trying to be funny."

"It's not that." He snatches a bag from my hand. "I was just thinking how you still sound like . . . you."

"I am still me. Just in different clothes. So, stop being weird." I move to grab my bag back, but he dodges out of my reach and somehow manages to steal the other one from me.

"Isa, for God's sake, let me try to be a gentleman," he says, heading for the backdoor with my bags.

"I didn't know you knew what that word meant." I chase after him, smirking.

"I learned it ten seconds ago when I took your bags," he quips, flashing me a haughty smile from over his shoulder as he opens the door. "Don't think this is all out of the kindness of my heart, though. I'm mostly doing it so you'll give me my present." He pauses, waiting for me to confirm if I got him a present like he asked.

I want to tell him no, just so I don't have to witness that cocky smile I know he's going to give me, followed by an *Ah-ha! I knew you liked me.*

But I did get him something while on my trip.

When I remain silent, his face lights up. "I knew you'd get me one." His grin expands. "Just like I knew you liked me."

"It's not that great of a present," I try to sidetrack his attention off the meaning of my present. "So don't get too excited," I warn, but then sigh when he continues to bounce with excitement. "Fine. Take my bags upstairs, and I'll give it to you."

"Wow, that's pretty forward of you." He bites on his bottom lip, trying really hard not to laugh at me.

My damn traitor skin heats up again. "Stop being such a perv."

He giggles. Actually freakin' giggles. And it just might be the adorablest thing ever. But I'm not about to tell him that.

"You're setting yourself up with these," he says. "Jesus, Isa. What the heck happened to you while you were on that trip? You leave all innocent and come back with a dirty mouth."

I pinch him in the side again and he ends up dropping one of the bags, and it lands on my toe.

"Shit, I'm sorry." He sets the other bag down and reaches to touch me then pulls back. "Are you okay?"

I glance down at my boot. "I'm fine. Totally didn't feel a thing with the boots."

"Are you sure?"

I bob my head up and down, and he smiles tensely, fidgeting as he steps back from me.

Why is he acting like a squirrely weirdo?

"Come on." He picks up the bags, going right back to the chillaxed version of Kai. "I want to see what you got me."

Nobody's home. That's the first thing I notice when I walk in. I'm not surprised my family isn't here to welcome me home, but it still hurts and makes me want to find my real mom even more.

Kai finds his own way to my room through my house, with me tailing at his heels. I'm surprised he remembers where everything is, since he hasn't been here for five years. But he navigates through the hallways easily and makes it to my room.

The moment he steps inside, though, he frowns. "What happened to all your posters and drawings?"

Confused, I scramble inside to see what he's talking about. The moment I catch sight of the bare and freshly painted white walls, my jaw collides with the floor. "I don't . . ." I yank my fingers through my hair as I turn in a circle. "Someone took all my stuff down.

"You didn't take them down?" Kai asks, dropping the bags onto my bed.

I shake my head as tears burn in my eyes. "They were here when I left. I don't know what happened."

But really, I do. Either my mom took them down, or

it was Hannah's form of revenge. Neither is a good alternative, because both probably mean all my posters and drawings are gone forever.

What if they're gone? What if I never see some of that stuff again? As depressing as it is, that stuff was a huge part of my life, especially my drawings.

Reality knocks the wind out of me, and a few tears manage to escape from my eyes.

"Hey, it's going to be okay," Kai says when he notices the waterworks.

I feel stupid, like a loser again, who cries over ridiculous drawings and posters, because they mean more to her than they should. "I'm sorry." I wipe away the tears with the back of my hand. "This is so stupid. I shouldn't be crying over drawings, especially in front of you."

"Hey, I cry too," Kai assures me, pressing his hand to his heart. "And I've cried over drawings and posters before."

"In front of people?" I question, and he hesitates. "See? That's the difference between you and me. You're not crazy enough to cry in front of other people who could eventually use it against you."

"I'm not going to use this against you," he promises. "Seriously, Isa. I'm not that big of an asshole."

"Sometimes you kind of are, though, to me anyway. With everyone else, you're usually so chill, but with me . . . it's like you get your kicks and giggles out of making me uncomfortable."

He rubs his hand across his jawline, considering something. "Okay, I'll admit I tease you a lot, but only because I'm comfortable around you." When I stare at him in disbelief, he adds, "Well, more comfortable around you than most people." He sighs when I still keep looking at him with skepticism. "Look, when I'm around other people,

I'm different—I know this. But everyone expects me to be this intense, serious guy all the time, like Kyler is."

"I hate to break it to ya, but Kyler's not that intense and serious all the time," I say, remembering how much he laughed when we spent those few weeks shooting hoops and hanging out.

Kai rolls his eyes. "Oh, please. The guy never, ever cracks a joke. Seriously, he's like the most serious person I've ever met, and honestly, he's kind of fucking boring. And you should hear him talk about sports. Talk about a snorefest." He bobs his head back and lets out a snore, emphasizing his point.

I try not to laugh, because he's making fun of Kyler, and it shouldn't be funny, yet a strangled laugh flees from my mouth.

Kai grins at the sound. "See? Deep down, you agree with me. You just don't want to admit it."

"I don't agree with you," I insist. "Kyler's not boring. He's just quiet and shy."

He makes a choking, gurgling sound then gapes at me. "Kyler's not shy at all, Isa. He's the most arrogant, self-assured asshole I've ever met."

"He might be that way to you," I say. "But to me, he seems quiet and nice."

"Wrong again. He's not nice. Not when you know him like I do." His features harden as he shakes his head in irritation. "My life would've been so much easier if he'd gone farther away for college, but no, he had to go here so he could remind me daily who the better Meyers is."

Hmm . . . perhaps Kai's one-eighty transformation might have had something to do with his brother.

"Okay, I get you're not a fan of your brother." I tread with caution, because I don't want to hurt his feelings, but at the same time, I feel bitter over how Kai treated me in seventh grade. While Kyler hasn't been my best friend or anything, he's always been nice to me, said hi to me in the hallways, and always stands up for me while I'm being picked on. Kai, on the other hand, spends most of his time teasing me, and he's never offered me an apology for telling his friend I was a stalker. "But Kyler's been nice to me."

"I've been nicer to you more than he has." He shifts his weight, seeming uneasy about something. Perhaps how he treated me in the past? I'll never know, since he won't say anything about it aloud. "Maybe not all the time, but definitely more than he has."

"You've also been mean to me more than he has, too." My hands shake as I remember the day he ripped out my heart and stomped on it.

"Most of the time, I'm just teasing you." His voice is a drop unsteady as he tiptoes around the big, ugly elephant in the room. "And I only do that, because I'm comfortable around you and you don't expect anything from me." He shrugs, offering me a small, oddly sheepish smile. "You treat me like a normal guy. You never use me to get to my brother." Another shrug, like that's that.

So, he definitely has issues with Kyler. But now that I think about it, I'm not that surprised. Kai always has kind of lived in Kyler's shadow when it comes to sports and girls and grades. It's not like he's not good at any of those things. It's just that he's always one step behind Kyler, almost perfect, but not quite.

But he's way funnier.

Maybe I should tell him that.

Be nicer to him than he's been to me. Try to cheer him up like I used to.

"I'm going to stop you right there," he says. "Because

I can already see you trying to put me together, and no one can put me together, Isa. I'm all kinds of fucked up." He swings around me and backs for the doorway. "And you still owe me a present for carrying your bags up the stairs. You better make sure to bring it to school with you on Monday; otherwise, I'm going to have to start charging interest." He winks at me before turning on his heels and leaving my room.

The silence sets in as I take in the bare walls around me. "This is so depressing," I mutter. "There's no way I can look at this for the next nine months."

An idea smacks me in the head. One that will more than likely get me into trouble with my parents, but fuck it. I'm already on the permanent Hate List with them. Besides, I didn't work so hard to become a more confident person just to flush it down the toilet the moment I got home.

Chapter
TEN

The mural's going to take a while and requires way more paint supplies than I have. Plus, I'm not the most fantastic painter, but I do know someone who's an amazing artist.

I pick up my phone and call Indigo.

"Hey, I need a favor," I say after Indigo answers my call.

She yawns. "Dude, Isa, I love you to death, but I just laid down to take a nap."

"Sorry. I'll make it quick." I flop down on my unmade bed and stare up at my lame-ass, boring ceiling. "I need you to pick me up Monday after school then come over to my house and paint a mural on my wall."

I chose Monday because Hannah will be at college orientation, at least according to the calendar downstairs. And more than likely, my mom will go with her, which means I'll have the entire house to myself for a while.

"A mural?" Confusion laces her voice. "What are you

talking about?"

Sighing, I quickly explain to her what happened to my room while I was gone. By the time I'm finished, she's cursed about twenty times and called Lynn and Hannah some very creative names.

"Will you help me?" I ask after she stops freaking out.

"Of course I'll help you," she says, still sounding pissed off. "We're so going to do something badass."

"I have a couple of ideas actually."

"Good. Draw them up, and I'll see what I can do."

"Awesome. And thanks."

"No prob," she says then yawns again. "All right, now I have to go to sleep, or I'll be super pissy when you see me on Monday.

Laughing, I say goodbye, but I don't put the phone away. I have one more call to make before I do.

I punch in Grandma Stephy's number.

"You need me to come rescue you?" she asks the moment she picks up.

"Not yet, but I do need a favor." I chew on my thumbnail then force myself to stop, because it's going to ruin my nail polish. "I know you said to wait a few days and sit on it, but I'm ready to talk to my dad. I can't wait anymore. I need to know."

"Honey, I really think we should wait a couple of days. You never know. You might change your mind and decide to wait, at least until you go off to college and get out of that house."

"Someone painted my room while I was gone." I force down the lump in my throat. "And took down all of my posters and drawings. Everything that was me in this room is gone. I need to know what happened. It's all I have left."

"Isa, I'm so sorry. Goddammit, your family's a bunch

of assholes," she curses, but when she speaks again, she's calm. "You still have me, sweetie. You know that, right? Just because we're not on a trip together doesn't mean we can't spend time together."

"I know, but I really need to do this. Finding my mom . . . finding out why she gave me up . . . I need to know."

Seconds tick by before she says anything.

"All right, I'll call up your father and schedule a time for the three of us to have dinner next week at my place," she says. "He's going to know something's up, though. I'm going to have to lie to him, or he won't come over."

"Tell him that you found something of Grandpa's you think he might like," I suggest. "He's always had a soft spot for Grandpa."

"That's actually a good idea, but how am I supposed to get him to bring you over."

"Just say you want to see me. He's not going to argue. Not when Lynn will be more than glad to get a break from me."

"I feel so sneaky right now," she muses through a chuckle. "I like it."

"That's because you're crazy," I tell her, smiling for the first time in over a day.

"I know I am." She pauses. "But, Isa, please promise me that no matter what happens with this—no matter where this goes—you'll always come talk to me if anything's ever bothering you. I don't ever want you to feel like you're in this alone."

I press my lips together and nod, even though she can't see me. "I promise."

"Good girl," she says. "And remember, I love you."

"I love you, too."

By the time I hang up, I'm crying. I decide to let it

all out, because it's better than holding it in and letting it smother me.

Ten minutes later, my eyes are swollen, I have the hiccups, and mascara and eyeliner stain my cheeks. I go to the bathroom to wash my face and fix my makeup before going back to my room and forcing myself to think about something other than my mom.

I stare out the window at the house next door, wondering when I'll run into Kyler. Part of me wants to, while part of me would rather not, especially since he's probably dating Hannah.

As I leave the window, I hear the front door open, and the sound of voices fills the house. Suddenly, all my Kyler and mom worries go bye-bye as bigger, more wicked problems arise.

I think about staying in my room. Never going out. But eventually, I'll have to face them, so might as well rip off the Band-Aid now. Besides, maybe I can get to the bottom of where the hell my drawings ended up.

Mustering up every ounce of courage I gained on the trip, I square my shoulders and march downstairs. But when I enter the living room and see my dad, Lynn, and Hannah all chilling on the sofa, surrounded by tons of shopping bags, chatting about orientation, my confidence goes *see ya later.*

I start to turn around to leave, when I hear Hannah say, "What the hell happened to you?"

Summoning a deep breath, I turn around and face them. "Hey."

"Um . . ." Hannah stares at me with her jaw hanging to her knees, totally speechless.

I fight the urge to cross my arms and try to cover myself up. "So, yeah, I'm back."

"We can see that." Lynn stares at me with an

unwelcoming expression, and even though it doesn't seem possible, I swear her eyes carry more hatred for me than they ever have.

I hold her death glare, though, even if my insides are jiggling around like a bouncy house. *I know who you really are. Know where that look of hate comes from. Trust me, I get it. Dad cheated on you, and you hate me, but you know what? You had no right to treat me the way you did, and one day I'm going to let you know that.*

The longer I look at her, the more she grinds her teeth, until she finally removes her eyes from me and focuses on digging around in the shopping bags.

"You look," my dad scratches his head as he stares at me, "nice."

"Henry," Lynn warns, blasting him with a scowl that could kill. "I thought you said you had stuff to do for work."

"I do." His eyes linger on me a beat or two longer then he stands up and says to Lynn, "I'll be in the office if anyone needs anything." He crosses the room, patting me on the shoulder as he passes. "It's nice to have you back," he whispers before hurrying down the hallway to his office.

Lynn must have heard him, because her attention zeroes in on me. "So, *Isabella*," she says my name in the craziest way, like it's an insult. "I see you had a pretty fun trip and got yourself a little makeover."

"You could say that," I reply dryly, sensing a punch line coming.

Her face pinches as she purposefully takes in my outfit. "You should've taken my advice. Dresses don't suit you, hon."

Hannah snickers as she takes out a pair of high heels from a box. "Don't be an idiot, Mom. Nothing suits her."

"Be nice, Hannah," Lynn says, smiling. "She can hear us."

I roll my tongue inside my mouth. I won't cry. I won't. "What happened to my room?"

Lynn exchanges a fleeting glance with Hannah then looks back at me. "We decided to get it ready for when you move out next year. We're going to turn it into a guestroom."

My fingers curl inward and pierce into my palms. "Okay. But where did you put all of my drawings and posters."

"I threw them away." She pulls out a silver dress from one of the bags. "They weren't in the best condition anyway. Most of the corners of the posters were torn, and those drawings . . ." She lays the dress down. " . . . well, I've been telling you for years how much I don't like those drawings, and decided it was time for them to go." She looks at me with her hands in her lap, her back straight, trying to appear so proper, the innocent victim.

But she's not fooling me. I can see the evil villain hidden inside her, the one who hates me and has been trying to ruin my life for the last fourteen years. Maybe that's why I'm really here. Maybe she wanted to punish my dad for cheating on her by torturing me.

"Awesome. I've been meaning to redecorate anyway." I plaster on a smile that only grows when both their jaws drop.

I should feel more satisfied than I do. I mean, I finally struck them speechless. In the end, though, I have to return to my room, where all I have left is the suitcases of stuff I brought back with me on my trip. Sure, it could be worse. I could have nothing.

But I miss my drawings. I put a lot of time and effort into them. They were part of me and got me through some rough and brutal days. In a way, the people who starred in the comics were kind of like my friends. Plus, there was the woman. My sidekick. The one I dreamed was my mother. Those sketches are gone too, and even though I was never positive it was my mom in the drawings, I still feel like I lost a part of her.

Chapter
ELEVEN

I learn three things over the next couple of days while stuck at home:

1. Lynn and Hannah hate my new look, and have made it their mission to destroy any confidence I've gained.

2. The new look seems to have put some kind of confusion spell on my dad, because he keeps staring at me like he's trying to figure something out, but can't quite get there.

3. Hannah and Kyler broke up, something I learn when I hear the two of them arguing in the driveway while I'm out drawing on the balcony. From the sound of things, they were never really together to begin with.

"I told you I didn't want a serious girlfriend and that I needed to focus on football," Kyler says to her. "I told you that on our second date."

"And I told you I didn't give a shit," she growls. "You should have thought about that when you kissed me."

"I never meant for that kiss to happen. I told you . . . I was a little drunk."

It's too dark outside for me to see them, but I can hear how uncomfortable Kyler is through his edgy tone.

"I'm really sorry, Hannah, but we're not getting together." He tries to sound firm. "You have to let this go."

When he walks away, I hear Hannah mutter, "Like hell I'm going to let this go. No one rejects me."

I shake my head. Aw, the downfall of being spoiled. She's so used to getting her way she doesn't know how to handle it when she doesn't.

The next couple of hours, I stay outside on my balcony, getting lost in a drawing. I'm not even sure how much time goes by, but eventually, my hand starts to cramp up.

"Having fun up there?" Kai's voice floats up from somewhere down below.

Startled, I drop the pencil and lean forward to peer over the railing. "Where are you?"

He giggles like a girl, and I think he might be drunk. "I'm invisible."

I rest my arms on the railing, squinting through the dark until I make out his silhouette in the driveway just below my balcony. "You know, you once told me you wanted to have the superpower of invisibility. Do you remember that?"

"I do remember that," he fully admits. "I'm still working on getting that superpower, though."

"You'll never be invisible," I tell him. "You're just not that kind of guy."

"Hey, maybe I can be . . . I mean, look at you. You turned un-invisible."

I'm glad he can't see me as my skin warms. "I'm not un-invisible. Nice word choice, by the way."

"Thank you. And that's what you are. Un-invisible."

As he shuffles backwards, the moonlight hits his face and I can see the swaying in his movements.

"You're drunk, aren't ya?" I tease.

He holds up his fingers an inch apart. "Just a tiny, tiny bit."

"Were you at a party?"

"I was . . . but not one of those lame-ass parties Kyler always goes to. This party was my kind of party. Not his."

"Okay," I say, again sensing tension between Kyler and him.

"Maybe next time you can come," he says softly. "I mean, I know I'm not my brother or anything, but I can be fun."

I catch the underlying meaning of his words, but before I can get too worked up, he staggers toward the fence that divides out yards.

"See you at school tomorrow, Isa." He clumsily hops over the fence and trips up the steps to his house.

"Yeah, see ya." I gather my things and head inside, trying not to stress over the fact that school starts tomorrow, and I have to go through with my plan to actually try to make friends. But as I lie down in bed to go to sleep, I'm nothing but a bundle of nerves.

I've always walked to school, even after I turned sixteen. While Hannah got a brand new car and a pool party for her sweet sixteen, I got her old bike and a cupcake. And while I was glad just to get something, the old bike does me absolutely no good today as I walk to school in black velvet platforms, not made for pedals. Seriously, what was I thinking? Yeah, the shoes looked cute when I bought them, and they are, as Indigo put it, 'fucking ama-zing', paired with my knee high socks, denim shorts, and grey crop tee. But by the time I reach school, the killer shoes are filled with my blood.

I'm trying not to limp as I cross the crowded parking lot toward the entrance. I have my attention on my schedule that came in the mail while I was gone, my thumb is hitched through the handle of my bag, and the wind is threatening to ruin my hair. But I'm rocking a side braid with these cool hair rings in it, and I manage to make it safely inside school without a hair moving out of place.

I should probably look up as I start down the hallway, but I want a couple more moments to collect myself before I have to stroll past people who have either never noticed me, or noticed me too much, thanks to Hannah. Even though she's now at college, some of her younger friends are still hanging around somewhere and might be ready to make fun of me, and God knows what they're going to say about that stupid rumor Hannah spread at the beginning of the summer about me being in a mental institution.

"Great, I have math first period," I gripe to myself as I weave my way down the crowded hallway toward my locker with my eyes glued to the schedule. "I hate ma—"

A shiver shoots up my spine as someone grabs me by the waist. Their palms graze the sliver of space between my shirt and shorts, and I just about lose my shit, because I know there's no way it could be one of my kinda, sorta friends touching me like that.

"What the hell?!" I squeal, reeling around and jumping back.

Kai is standing there, wearing a pair of dark jeans, and a shirt for once—we are in school, after all. His hair is a mad mess, but in a bedhead sorta way, and he's biting his bottom lip, struggling not to laugh at me.

"What are you doing?" I hiss, shoving his shoulder.

"Clearly making a scene," he replies, his gaze skimming the hallway.

I glance behind me and cringe. Almost half the people standing near us are gawking, probably because I squealed like a rabid beast. Great. So much for making a good first day impression and not drawing attention to myself.

Facing Kai, I lightly shove him. "Dude, you can't just grab people like that. You scared the shit out of me."

"When I grab most girls like that, they like it," he says with a smirk.

"Well, I'm not most girls . . . and I'm not used to people touching me." I fidget with a bracelet on my wrist, feeling all sorts of jittery standing here, with half the damn school gawking at me. "You feeling better?"

His brows dip. "What do you mean?"

"I mean, better than you did last night. You were a little out of it."

His eyes widen. "I talked to you last night?"

I nod, loving how shocked I made him. "You did. You actually yelled up at my balcony just to get my attention. It was very *Romeo and Juliet*." I shoot him a grin so he'll know I'm kidding.

He crosses his arms and shifts his weights. "Did I say anything . . . I don't know . . . weird?"

When I shrug, he narrows his eyes at me.

"Nothing too weird. Well, other than you declared your undying love for me. Oh yeah, and for zombies." I smile when he grows even more uneasy. "Relax, you didn't say anything weird. Although, you did invite me to come to the next party with you."

"I did, huh?" He rubs his scruffy jawline, musing over something. "Interesting."

Silence stretches between us, and my thoughts wander back to the people watching us.

I wanted today to go great, but I already have blisters on my heels and screamed in front of half my class. Maybe Hannah was right with what she said to me this morning. "Once a freak. Always a freak," she sneered when she saw me all dressed up.

I shake my head. No. She's not right. I won't let her be.

I straighten my shoulders and prepare myself. Time to do this. Face the music. Walk in head-on. I just cross my fingers and toes that the majority of the people here have forgotten the rumor Hannah spread at the beginning of the summer, that I was being admitted to a mental institution.

"I have to figure out where all my classes are." I wave bye to Kai. "See ya later, maybe."

"You've been going here for three years, Isa. You know where all the classrooms are." He snags ahold of my arm and hauls me toward the stairway that leads to the second floor.

I shuffle after him, noting that people are still staring at us, either because they think I'm insane or because Kai has his hand on my arm. Sure, he's talked to me in school before, to tease me mainly, but he's definitely never dragged me up the stairway.

He doesn't let me go until we reach a locker toward the end of the hallway on the second floor. By the time his fingers leave my arm, my skin is tingling in the nicest way ever.

"What's with all the touching?" I ask him as I shift the handle of my bag higher onto my shoulder.

He shrugs as he twists the combination of his locker. "You're the one who let me do it."

"I didn't really have a choice."

"You always have a choice."

"Yeah, you're right." I anxiously glance around the hallway, noticing people are still eyeballing us with fascination. "But you've never done that in the past. I mean, held onto my arm in public. Or talked to me." I want to say so much more. Want to point out that back in the day, he wouldn't be caught dead with me. But this doesn't feel like the time or place to bring it up.

He opens his locker. "Actually, I have before. Or at least I tried to. But usually when I tried to drag you down the hallway to . . . what did you call it the other day?" His head tilts to the side as he smirks. "Oh, yeah, 'to get my kicks and giggles', you pulled away and ran away from me like I was on fire."

I cross my arms, feeling self-conscious. "That's because I knew you were making fun of me."

"No, that was all in your head." He taps his finger against my temple. "It's all psychological, but now that you're," he glances up and down at me, lingering extra long on the sliver of skin peeking out of my shirt, "yeah, now you're okay with it, because you're more okay with yourself."

"Is that why you brought me up here? Just to see if I'd come with you?" I ask curiously.

He smiles at me, and I playfully swat his arm.

He places a hand over his arm where I swatted him, laughing. "What's with all the abuse?"

"Sorry, but you're purposely trying to make me mad." I tuck my hands into the back pocket of my shorts. "Now, if you're done playing with my mind, I'm going to go track down my locker."

As I turn to leave, he catches the bottom of my shirt and tows me back to him. "I didn't just bring you up here to play with your mind," he says. "You owe me a gift."

"The gift. Yeah, I forgot about that." I slide my backpack off, unzip it, and dig out the small box his gift is in, taking my time just so I'll drive him crazy. When he reaches for the box in my hand, I tuck it behind my back. "Ask nicely."

His eyes narrow to slits, but it's a playful move. "Fine, Isa, can I pretty please," he juts out his bottom lip, "with cherries and sprinkles and caramel on top, have my present?"

"I'll give it to you, but only because of all the dessert references." I hand over the box.

"You know, you've been promising you're going to give it to me a lot lately." His lips quirk as he opens the box and takes out the leather bracelet engraved with his name on it.

I ignore his dirty remark, but my cheeks warm. "I got it while I was in Paris. I know it's not anything super awesome, but there was this guy on the street making them, and it made me think of you." I flick his wrist, where he already has an array of bracelets. "I wasn't even positive you'd still be wearing them by the time I got back, since you never used to up until . . ." I shrug, "well, you changed. I wasn't sure if this bad boy thing of yours was going to be a phase."

He looks up at me, his expression dead serious. "Is this hot girl thing of yours a phase?"

"It's not a hot girl phase," I promise him, although my tone's a little shaky. "And no, it's not a phase. But I do need to figure out some stuff."

"What kind of stuff?"

"I don't know. Just stuff."

He stares at me just long enough to make me uneasy then drops the gaze to the bracelet as he ties it to his wrist.

"I like it."

"You don't have to like it." But I kind of want him to. "Although, it was way better than the painting my cousin tried to talk me into getting you. You don't seem like a painting kind of guy."

He flicks the bracelet on his wrist. "This is way, way better than a painting." He smiles at me, a genuine smile. "But you know what this means, right? You liiiike me."

Biting back a smile, I shake my head. "It so does not."

"Does too."

"Oh, fine. Whatever."

"Ha! I won that round."

"Only because I let you."

He's grinning from ear to ear. "I like this." He points back and forth between the two of us. "We should do this more often."

"Do what more often?" I ask.

Before he can respond, Braden, one of his stoner friends, strolls up to Kai.

"Hey, did you bring that thing we were talking about the other night at that party?" he asks, stuffing his hands into his pockets.

Kai glances at me, and Braden tracks his gaze. He blinks, either stunned or high—it's hard to tell for sure, because his eyes are really, really bloodshot.

"Hey," he says, blinking again as he checks me out, "I know you, right?"

I shake my head, trying not to squirm from his attentive gaze. "Probably not."

Kai rubs the back of his neck and tensely glances around the hallway. I know what's coming. Like the time he was caught walking home with me, he's going to make some lame-ass excuse of why he's here with me.

"I'll see you later," I say, deciding to let him off the

hook.

Before anyone can say anything else, I turn around and walk back toward the stairway. As I make my way downstairs, I notice that fewer people are looking in my direction, but some still stare. I ignore the gawking the best I can, but by the time I make it to my locker, I feel sick to my stomach. I have no idea how I'm going through with my plan of making some real friends, when I can barely handle people staring.

Give it time. You'll get used to it.

That's what I try to tell myself through my morning classes and during lunch, when I sit at the same corner table by myself, like I did the previous three years. I get desperate enough that I try to spot Kai at one of the tables, but he must leave campus for lunch, because I don't see him anywhere. I end up eating lunch while texting Indigo, so I won't have to deal with the staring plague that seems to have taken over my school.

I'm not positive what's causing the gawking. I haven't heard any gossip that includes my name and my mental stability, so I don't think the rumor is causing people to act crazy. Still, the thought hovers there in the back of my mind. What if they all think I'm insane? Do I care? I don't want to, and the Isa who was overseas wouldn't, but being back at home, where everyone knows the real me, I kind of do.

By the time the final bell rings, I've made a total of zero friends, and strangely, the handful of people I did talk to during my junior year won't even look me in the eye.

Frustrated, I hurry out of the school, pushing my way through the mob of people on the sidewalk. As I reach the parking lot, my phone buzzes from inside my pocket, so I dig it out.

Indigo: Dude, I forgot how lame high school is.

Me: What r u talking about? You're at school? What school?

Indigo: I'm talking about the lameness of your high school and all high schools in general.

Me: R u here?

Indigo: Duh. How could I not come pick u up after all those depressing texts u sent me?

My gaze lifts to the parking lot and I spot her, sitting on the trunk of my grandma's car, with her hair pulled up in a bun, smoking a cigarette. I run to her. I don't even care how crazy I look at the moment. I'm just so damn glad she's here.

She hops off the trunk, and I hug the bejesus out of her. "So, I'm guessing by the crazy hugging that your first day totally sucked?" she says as she hugs me back.

"It was awful," I tell her. "Everyone kept staring, and even my old friends wouldn't talk to me. The only person who said anything to me at all was Kai, and that's because he wanted his present."

"Aw, Kai." The tone of her voice implies something. "He wouldn't happen to be around, would he?"

I move back and eye her over suspiciously. "Why?"

She shrugs, dropping her cigarette to the ground and stomping it out with the tip of her boot. "I'm just curious. I mean, other than Kyler, he's the only person from Sunnyvale I've heard you mention. And you're in love with Kyler, so it makes sense why you talked about him, but with Kai," she bobs her head back and forth, wavering, "I want to find out why he's always so stuck in your head."

"He's not stuck in my head. I talk about him, because he's, like, one of the few people who's ever talked to me at school, and that was only on rare occasions." I frown as she stubbornly keeps looking at all the people walking by us. "And I have no idea where he is. I haven't seen him since this morning." I head for the passenger side of the car. "Please tell me you're taking me for ice cream, because I'm in desperate need of some sugar."

Her back stiffens. "We actually need to go straight to Grandma's."

I grasp the door handle. "Why? Is everything okay?"

She won't look me in the eye, which is completely out of character for her. "Something happened between her and your dad. They got in a fight and . . ."

"And what?" I press.

She sighs, meeting my gaze. "And she got a name out of him."

"She did. Yes!" I fist pump the air then hop into the car, bubbling with excitement. Holy shit, she has a name. A freaking name. I'm so excited I can't sit still.

Indigo climbs into the car and turns on the engine. "Isa, I don't want you to get too excited. Grandma may have gotten a name, but your dad wouldn't tell her anything else. And he's super pissed. Like, really, really angry." She backs out of the parking space. "He even broke a vase."

"That doesn't matter." All that matters is I'm about to learn my mother's name. I can do a lot with a name. I can even track her down if I want to, without my dad's help, which I plan on doing.

Because like I promised myself in Paris, I'm going to find her, no matter what it takes.

Chapter
TWELVE

Thirty minutes later, Indigo is parking the car in front of Grandma Stephy's apartment. I have so much pent up energy inside me that I jump out of the car before it comes to a complete stop. I've done the ninja move before, but never in four-inch platforms, and I end up rolling my ankle and eating asphalt as I fall to the ground.

"For the love of God." I clumsily push to my feet and look at the damage. My knee is bleeding and pebbles are stuck in the open cut. I think a piece of glass might be in there too. I almost throw up. I'm cool with seeing blood and gore on television, but it's a whole different story when the blood's gushing out of me. But determined to make it inside, I force the vomit back and pluck out the glass.

"Oh, my God . . ." Oxygen is ripped from my lungs as more blood trickles out of the wound.

"Jesus, Isa, are you okay?" Indigo rushes around the front of the car toward me.

"I'm totally fine." *I can do this. Be tough.* I take off, limping up the sidewalk toward my grandma's place.

"Isa, would you please slow down?" Indigo's sandals scuff against the ground as she jogs to catch up with me. "You're leaving a trail of blood all over the ground, for God's sake."

I look down and, sure enough, blood is dripping out of the cut, down my leg, and onto the concrete. I gag, but fuse my lips together.

"Holy shit, I think you might need stitches," Indigo remarks as she bends over and squints at the open wound.

"The stitches can wait until I talk to Grandma." I hobble toward the apartment again, refusing to look down at the cut.

Cotton candy. Gummy worms. Licorice. I chant in my head, trying to stay calm.

"You're going to end up with a scar if you don't take care of it," Indigo points out, stopping by the front door to light up.

"I'll take care of it." I open the apartment door and stumble into Grandma Stephy's living room.

She's sitting on the couch, surrounded by tons of used Kleenexes, and her head is in her hands. When I enter, she quickly looks up, blinking her puffy eyes.

"Oh, my God, I'm so sorry." She stands up and winds around the coffee table toward me. "I think I messed up."

"Indigo says you got a name. Please tell me that's true." I hunch over and place my hand on my knee.

Now that the adrenaline rush is fading, the pain is becoming way more knock-me-on-my-ass intense and the vomit burning at the back of my throat is harder to keep down.

"He accidentally let it slip out when he was yelling at me," she says with a cautious edge to her voice. "But I'm not even sure he realized he said it."

Unable to stand any longer, I sink down on the floor and straighten my knee. "What happened, anyway? Why was he even here? I thought we were going to do this together?" I blink a few times as everything around me spins.

"Honey, what did you do to your leg?" She kneels down on the carpet beside me to examine the cut on my knee. "My word, Isa. This looks really, really bad."

"I jumped out of the car and fell." I slump back, resting my head against the door. "Please, Grandma Stephy, just tell me her name." Breathe in. Breathe out. Breathe through the pain.

"Her name is Bella," my grandma says right before I pass out.

When my eyelids flutter open, my eyes are instantly assaulted by florescent light, the smell of cleaner attacks my nostrils, and my knee feels like a zombie took a bite out of it.

"Where the hell am I?" I mutter as I sit up.

"Easy, Isa." My grandma Stephy appears by my bedside, looking paler than normal. "We had to take you to the hospital."

I take in the privacy curtain, the thin bed I'm lying in, and Indigo sitting in a chair. "How'd I get . . ." I cup my head then my mouth sinks. "Oh . . ." The last few hours rush back to me.

Grandma Stephy pats my hand that's resting on my stomach. "You've never been good with blood, but you worried me to death when you blacked out."

I look down at my knee, which is now wrapped in a

bandage—thank God. "Did I have to get stitches?"

"You did." Grandma Stephy smoothes my hair from my forehead so she can look me in the eyes. "How are you feeling? About *everything*?"

"The leg hurts," I admit. "And the thing with my mom . . . you said her name was Bella." I smile at that. "I have to be named after her, right?"

"I guess so." Grandma Stephy glances over her shoulder at Indigo. "Honey, would you mind going and getting me a soda from the vending machine?"

Indigo nods and Grandma Stephy waits until she ducks out from the curtain before she sits down on the edge of the bed. "Isa, your dad knows I told you about your mom. That's why he came over to my house today."

"But how did he find out? I didn't say anything to him."

"You didn't have to. He said he knew from the moment you got back from your trip. He said you looked so much like her, and he just jumped to the conclusion that your change came from learning who your mom is."

"I look like her?" I try not to act too giddy, because Grandma Stephy seems upset, but I can't help it. I'm totally freakin' excited.

"According to your dad, you do." She dazes off into empty space. "I can't believe how your father acted today. I mean, I always kind of knew he was a spoiled brat, but . . ." She looks at me. "Your grandpa used to spoil him all the time, because he was his only son. Everything Henry wanted, your grandpa gave him. I knew one day it would backfire, but the way he treated me," she shakes her head, "I just can't believe that man yelling at me today is my son."

"I'm sorry. I feel like this is all my fault."

"It's not your fault. He never should've kept you in

the dark like he did. But what I don't get is how on Earth he thought I told you how your mother looked, and all the other stuff he was saying. He acted like I somehow found out everything about her and told you."

"Maybe he thought you hired a private investigator." I shift my leg into a more comfortable position as the low ache ignites into a fiery pain.

"Maybe." She mulls over something, tousling her short hair with her fingers. "I don't know, though. I'd have to have a starting point for that, which I don't."

"But there has to be a starting point. I mean, if she had me and I lived with her for a while, it'd be document-ed, like say with a birth certificate."

"You sound like a mystery novel right now, Isa," she says with a thoughtful smile.

"Well, I do read them a lot," I admit. "But I'm just saying, her name has to be on it, doesn't it?"

She promptly shakes her head. "I know where you're going with this, and the answer is no."

I give her my most innocent look, my lips parting, my eyes widening. "I have no idea what you're talking about."

"Your father is already upset as it is," she contin-ues, ignoring me. "If he caught you snooping around," she shakes her head in dismay, "I don't even want to go there."

"He's not going to hurt me, if that's what you're thinking."

"I know he won't hurt you, but with how they treat you now, and if Lynn gets involved in this . . ." She sighs heavily as she checks the screen of her phone. "I really think you should reconsider my offer to come live with me. Your father won't be happy about it, but that doesn't mean I can't fight it. He's proved way too many times that he doesn't deserve to have you around."

"I don't think he'd care," I say, repositioning my leg.

"I wouldn't be so sure of that," she tells me with a heavy-hearted look. "In fact, he might have mentioned something about me staying away from you while he was mad. And he's probably going to yell at me when he gets here."

My mouth curves to a frown as my shoulders slump. "He's headed here? Why?"

"Because he's your guardian and you're on his insurance." She covers her hand over mine. "Don't worry. He's just going to be angry with me."

"Well, I'm going to let him know this is all my fault." I grip her hand, trying to tell myself that everything will be okay. "I'm sure once he realizes that, he'll let me see you again." Besides, there's no way Lynn would ever let my dad try to keep me at our house.

"I'm not sure he's going to change his mind about this. Usually, I'd say yes—that his threat was one of his temper tantrums—but this time he seemed pretty dead set on you keeping your distance from me." Determination fills her eyes. "I can make it happen, Isa. Just say you want to live with me, and I'll make sure to get you out of that house."

I take in her kind eyes that have dark circles under them, and her pale skin. She looks way more worn out than the Grandma Stephy I know. The fight she had with my dad today must've gotten to her more than she's letting on.

"I'm fine," I assure her as confidently as I can. "Besides, I don't want to have to change schools and be known as the new girl for my senior year."

"You never know. Being the new girl might give you a chance at a fresh start, which was what you and

Indigo were always yammering about during the trip. Every damn night, that's all I heard while I was trying to fall asleep." She tries to appear annoyed, but a trace of a smile forms at her lips.

She's right. Starting a new school could give me a fresh start, and hey, maybe I'd even make some new friends and no longer have to be Loner Girl. But putting more stress on Grandma Stephy is definitely something I don't want to do.

"Can we talk about me living with you in a couple of weeks? Maybe after my dad's cooled off, he might be more willing to agree to let me go." I'm almost certain he will. It's not like he wants me there anyway.

"Maybe." She sounds pretty skeptical, though, which makes me wonder exactly what was said during their argument. Her shoulders slump forward as she sighs. "If that's what you want. But only if you promise to call me the moment things get too bad."

Things have been bad for years now, but I don't point that out. "All right, I promise." And just because I know it'll make her smile, I stick out my pinkie. "In fact, I pinkie swear."

She shakes her head, but her smile breaks through and she hitches her pinkie with mine.

The moment we pull away, my dad comes storming in.

"Get. Out." He looks at Grandma Stephy as he points toward the exit. "Now."

"Watch your tongue, young man." Grandma Stephy collects her purse from a chair and slings the handle over her shoulder. "You might think it's okay to talk to your mother like this, but it's not. You will respect me."

"I'll respect you as much as you respect me," he growls, stepping toward her. "Telling Isa what you did.

You had no right."

"I'm not going to get into this with you again," she replies as calmly as she can. "I'm going to go home, and I'll call you in a few days when you've calmed down."

"Don't call ever again," he shouts after her as she walks out of the room. "And you're never to see Isa again."

"Dad, stop," I hiss. "Leave Grandma alone. She didn't do anything wrong."

My dad's attention whips back to me and, by the anger in his eyes, I expect him to yell at me. But when he speaks, he's unsettling composed. "We're not going to talk about this ever again. No mention of it, okay?"

I shake my head. "No. I'm going to mention it. A lot. And I'm going to bug you until you tell me who my mom is."

He ignores me, his back as stiff as a board. "I'm going to go get the doctor."

Before I can get another word out, he leaves the room.

I grit my teeth, more furious than I've ever been. I make another vow to myself right then and there that the second I get home, I'm going to get my hands on my birth certificate.

Chapter
THIRTEEN

Okay, so I might have been too confident at the hospital about how easy it was going to be to get ahold of my birth certificate. I've been searching the house for days and haven't stumbled across it yet. I did find Hannah's in a trunk in my parent's room, so logically it seemed like mine should be in there too. But nope. Not even my social security card was in there. I even tried looking for information on the Internet, but all that came up under my name was my blog and the last entry I made on it, where I broke down and rambled on about my search for my mother.

I thought about deleting the post right after I wrote it, but since I have three followers and none of them are from around here—except for Grandma Stephy—I decided it's okay to leave it up. Plus, it felt kind of good to talk about it aloud . . . well, aloud in a way.

To add more complication to my life, Lynn and my dad have gone into Isabella Doesn't Exist Mode. They refuse to acknowledge when I'm in the room, when I speak, or even when I 'accidentally' dropped a glass cup on the floor to try to get their attention. My dad did make eye contact with me a couple of times, but mostly he just stares at me like he's seen a ghost. The look is honestly creeping me out.

If it weren't for Hannah, I'd seriously believe I somehow got ahold of an invisibility cape and am unintentionally wearing it. But she lets me know I still exist in the visible realm, in a very, very Hannah-like way.

"What's up with those god awful shoes?" she asks Saturday morning as I enter the kitchen to get some breakfast. She's wearing her pajamas with no makeup on and her hair's a mess.

I glance down at the flip-flips on my feet. "I have to wear flats because of this." I point to the bandage on my knee that covers the stitches.

"You look fucking stupid. Like you're going to the beach or something, which is just dumb since we live in the mountains and it's September. Plus, you really need a mani/pedi if you're going to wear stuff like that," Hannah sneers as she breaks apart a granola bar. Once it's in half, she reads the side of the box. "So that makes it seventy-five calories," she mutters to herself.

All the things I wish I could say to her burn at the tip of my tongue, but I bite them back, mostly because I'm not in the mood to war with her.

While she's calorie counting, I steal a vanilla cupcake from the platter on the kitchen island and a soda from the fridge. As I'm hurrying out of the room, her eyes zero in on me.

"Ew, is that what you're eating for breakfast?" she says, glaring at the cupcake in my hand. "You're going to get fat if you eat like that."

"I always eat like this." I lick a huge glob of frosting off the top of the cupcake. "It's so yummy."

She practically drools as she eyeballs the delicious treat in my hand, and I find it oddly satisfying, knowing she wants to eat the cupcake, but won't.

"Good luck keeping the weight off," she hollers after me as I dash out of the kitchen. "Oh yeah, and Isa!"

"So close," I mumble to myself. Then I lean back and pop my head into the kitchen. "Yeah?"

"Mom and Dad wanted me to tell you something." She drums her manicured nails against the granite countertop. "Hmmm . . . I think it was important, but I can't remember what it is." A smirk curls at her lips. "Oh, I remember. They told me to tell you that they loved you, to be safe, and that if you need anything to call them."

"They did?" I ask then a second later realize my mistake. But it's too late. She's already grinning like the Cheshire Cat.

"Oh, wait," she says with a fake laugh. "That message was for me. Not you." She stands up from the barstool with half a granola bar in her hand. "They wanted me to remind you that you're not allowed to see Grandma Stephy, and to make sure to clean the entire house while they're gone." She skips out of the kitchen, intentionally bumping me into the wall as she passes by me.

I'm unsure if she's telling the truth or not, but I'd be lying if it didn't gut me apart. I hate that there's a huge chance she's not lying.

By the time I make it to my room, my eyes are watery, my chest aches with loneliness, and I've wolfed down most of the cupcake. I pop the tab on the soda and take a swig before setting the can down on the nightstand. Then I stare at my plain white walls that are patched up from all the tacks and nails I used to hold up my drawings and posters. Indigo has yet to make it over to paint the mural, because we haven't really gotten a chance. I know if my parents are around when she comes over they'll put a stop to our painting and punish me big time. If I do paint it while they're gone, it'll take them some time to discover what I've done, since they've gone back to never coming up to my room.

I decide to text Indigo so we can put the mural plan in motion, since my parents are on vacation for the weekend.

> *Me: Hey, u wanna come over and paint my wall or what?*

> *Indigo: Sorry! Can't today. I have a job interview.*

I'm mildly bummed, but super excited for her.

> *Me: Where?!*

> *Indigo: At that art gallery I told u about.*

> *Me: Yay! I'll keep my fingers crossed for u.*

> *Indigo: U better. If I get this job then I can get my own place. No offense to Grandma Stephy, but I'm getting a little tired of Friday night poker at the community center. Plus, that Harry dude has been coming over a lot. I seriously can't look either one of them in the eye when they're together.*

> *Me: LOL. I still can't believe we walked in on them.*

> *Indigo: I wish I could forget . . . the sounds . . . they still haunt my nightmares.*

> *Me: But she seems happy with this Harry dude, right?*

> *Indigo: She really does.*

Me: Good. I want her to be happy. And fingers and toes crossed u get the job!

Indigo: Thanx! Let u know when I do. Rain check on the room painting.

Me: Yep! Might go get paint supplies today, since I don't have anything else to do.

Other than look for my birth certificate. But I'm honestly running out of places to look. There's only one thing I can think of to do and that's confront my dad. But I'm not sure if he'll even acknowledge me asking.

"When they get back from their trip, I'm going to ask my dad if I can go move in with Grandma Stephy, and then I'm going to confront him," I tell myself with fierce determination. "But right now, I'm going to go get some paint . . . give myself a little break from this house and this room." I pull a face at the walls as I grab some cash from my nightstand drawer from a stash I collected over the years. Most of it came from my grandpa. Every holiday and birthday, he'd give me a card with at least ten bucks in it.

"For college," he said simply. "Or just a rainy day."

I glance out my window at the raindrops beading the glass. "Perfect, a rainy day." I tuck a few twenties into my back pocket then stuff the rest back in the drawer and collect my jacket from my closet.

I zip up my jacket and head out in my shorts and flip-flops. I'm going to seriously freeze my butt off, but I've done the walk to town in sun, rain, and snow before and lived. My outfit isn't that fashionable or practical for cold weather. Pulling skinny jeans over my knee is like trying to stuff Indigo's and my movie candy stash into a purse, which never, ever worked—we both have serious sweet tooth issues.

Luckily, I hit the sister jackpot, because Hannah's no-where in sight as I head downstairs. If she were, she'd be all over my shorts and hoodie combo.

When I reach the backdoor, I wrap my fingers around the doorknob, count to the three, and barrel outside.

Cold rain instantly soaks through my clothes as I skip down the driveway, moving awkwardly, because I can't bend one knee. I don't care though. Rain is awesome. And it smells so great. Seriously, if I could, I'd skip around in the rain all the time.

My hair is drenched by the time I reach the side-walk, and the flip-flops splash water from the puddles all over the backs of my legs. It reminds me of this one time Kai and I walked home in the rain and we intentionally splashed in all the puddles.

"Isa! What are you doing?!" Someone shouts with a hint of laughter in their voice.

My head whips to the side as I stumble to a stop.

Kai is standing out on the side deck, beneath the shelter of the roof, and I think he might be laughing at me, but the veil of rain crashing from the cloudy sky makes it difficult to see.

"Going to the paint store!" I shout then wave at him and start to skip off again.

"Are you crazy?" he calls out. "You can't walk to town in the middle of a rainstorm."

I sigh and slow down again. "I'm not walking! I'm skipping!" My eyelashes flutter against the rain.

"Can't you wait until it at least stops raining?" he asks, shaking his head as I jump into a puddle.

"No way! It's either the rain or being in the house with Hannah. And I choose the rain. Besides, rain is awesome!"

I can hear him laughing all the way from over here.

"Would you get your ass over here?" He waves at me to come to him. "I'll drive you if you really want to go. But it's too damn cold for you to be playing around in the rain, no matter how cute you look."

Cute? Did he just call me cute? No, I must've heard him wrong.

I don't go over there right away. Ever since the first day of school, Kai and I haven't really talked that much. But he's also skipped out on a lot classes, and the few times he has made a grand appearance, he seems exhausted and out of it. I don't want to jump to conclusions like the rest of the town, but it's almost like he wants people to think he's a troublemaker.

"Would you stop overthinking and get your ass over here?" he yells at me, smiling as he leans over the railing.

"Oh, fine. Take away my rain fun." I hike up his driveway and dive underneath the shelter of the porch.

"That's a nice look for you. Totally weather appropriate too," he teases as he gives a once over to my drenched shorts, jacket, and hair. The black shirt, dark jeans, and a studded belt he's wearing make him look like he's trying to go Goth. This isn't his normal look, so I wonder if he's going somewhere or just taking his bad boy image to a new level.

I wring my hair out. "I can't wear anything else other than shorts and sandals until my knee heals; otherwise, the stitches hurt."

"Stitches?" He frowns. "What happened?"

"I jumped out of a moving car and fell on a piece of glass." I shrug like it's no big deal.

"Very badass." He stares at me long enough to make my insecurity go up about a thousand notches. "I was actually just teasing you about your clothes. Although, you definitely pull off the wet clothes look." He tugs on a wet strand of my hair and dazzles me with a lopsided smile. "Relax, Isa. I'm not making fun of you. Never have." His smile broadens. "And you look fine in wet clothes. But cold." He nods at the door. "Come on. Let's get you inside."

I wrap my arms around myself as I shiver. "I am kinda freezing my ass off." My teeth clank together as the chattering sets in. "But don't worry, I'm tough."

"I know you are." He winks at me for God knows what reason. I must give him a funny look, because he laughs and says, "Relax, I don't bite," before opening the door.

We step inside the washroom and I slip off my shoes so I won't track mud all over the hardwood floors.

"You should take your jacket off too," Kai says as he shuts the door. "My mom is weird about us tracking water through the house."

Nodding, I unzip my jacket and slip my arms out of my sleeves. Kai watches me from the doorway like I'm the most fascinating thing in the world as I hang it up on the hook near the door. Thankfully, my shirt's fairly dry, and after losing the cold, wet jacket, my body temperature starts to warm up again.

"So . . ." I wrap my arms around myself more. I've never been in his house before, and I feel so nervous. "You said you could take me to the store."

He nods, backing through the doorway and into the kitchen with his eyes on me. "I can give you a ride when I head out to a party if you want."

"Okay," I confusedly follow him into the kitchen, "but that means I'd have to walk home." I hold up my hands when he arches a brow at me. "Which is totally fine by me."

He scoops up an apple from a basket on the counter. "It'll probably be late when I head out. I'm not sure it's a good idea for you to be walking around in the rain *while* it's late."

"Um . . ." Okay, I so don't get guys. Didn't he offer to take me to the store? So why does it sound like he doesn't want to now? "I guess I can just walk there right now then."

He bites into the apple and studies me while chewing. "Or, you could just go with me."

"To a *party* with *you*."

He chuckles, wiping juice from his chin with his sleeve. "You don't have to sound so disgusted when you say it. I promise I'm not that gross." He wavers, bobbing his head from side to side. "Now the party on the other hand, I'm not going to make any promises."

"I don't think you're gross. I'm just confused."

"Over?"

"Over you inviting me to one of your parties. I mean, I know you said that when you were drunk, but I didn't think you were serious."

"I was—am. And it's not my party. It's Bradon's." He takes another bite of the apple. "You know. That guy you met at my locker."

"Yeah, I remember," I say, trying not to think about how he blew me off the moment Bradon showed up.

"Something's up," Kai accuses, eyeing me down. "You have a tone."

I shrug, feigning dumb. "That's just how my voice sounds."

"No, it doesn't." He sinks his teeth into the apple again. "You don't like Bradon."

"I don't even know Bradon, other than the two seconds we met at your locker."

"Then what's with the tone?"

I chew on my bottom lip and shrug.

He gives me a stern look. "Isa, don't make me get it out of you."

I roll my eyes. "You say that like you have the power to actually make me. And you don't, unless you're secretly a wizard."

He smashes his lips together, suppressing a laugh. Then, with his gaze trained on me, he sets the apple down on the counter and cracks his knuckles. "I do know how to make you, even if I don't have magic powers. Well, unless you've become less ticklish over the last five years." He bedazzles me with an arrogant grin as I step away from him.

"You promised me when I told you my kryptonite that you'd never use it against me," I gripe as I take another step back. But this time, he matches my move, stealing the space I put between us. "Kai, I'm serious. You promised you wouldn't ever tickle me."

"I don't remember making such a promise."

"Oh, yeah, well . . ." I frantically search for a way to stop him.

"I don't know why you're acting so scared. There's nothing to get scared about. It's just a little tickling." He innocently bats his eyelashes at me

"Oh yeah, well . . . FYI, you just fluttered your eyelashes like a girl." I know it's a lame attempt to get him to stop, but it's all I've got at the moment.

Of course, he finds my attempt more amusing than annoying, and even laughs. I narrow my eyes at him, trying to think of a better insult, but I'm blindsided as he barrels at me with his fingers ready to attack my sides.

"Kai! Stop!" I squeal, hunching over and trying to protect my sides with my arms. I snort a big old pig laugh as he tickles the air out of me. "If you don't stop, I'm go-ing to tell everyone at school that you know what kryp-tonite is and that you used to want to be Superman."

"That was in the seventh grade." He continues tick-ling me. "That stuff doesn't matter anymore."

I swing around him and skitter around the kitchen island, but he catches the back of my shirt. "So, you just outgrew that phase then, huh?" I ask between my laughs as he drags me back toward him.

"No, I still think it'd be pretty cool to be Superman." His fingers dig into my sides, his chest is pressed against my back, and his warm breath is brushing the back of my neck. "I just don't give a shit if anyone finds that out anymore."

When his fingers stop moving, I peek up at him. "You're saying that you've changed since seventh grade? That you're not that guy anymore who wants to be so popular?" I roll my eyes just to bug him.

"I'm not even close to that guy anymore," he prom-ises me, with his hands on my waist. "And it's not that crazy to change over five years. You changed over three months."

"Okay, I get your point, I guess, but it's still kind of hard to believe you've changed that much." This time, I do have a tone.

He sighs heavily. "Isa, I really am sorry I was a dick to you back then. I know it's not an excuse, but I was dealing with a lot of shit, and . . ." He shrugs, which looks awkward, since he still has his hands on me and his chest aligned with my back. "I've wanted to apologize to you for a while, but every time I say anything to you, you'd act like I was the most annoying person in the world. But I get it. I totally deserve for you to treat me like that."

"You can be the most annoying person in the world,"

I joke, but my emotions get the best of me and my voice cracks. "It's okay, I guess. I mean, I get it. We were different people back then."

"It's not okay. And I'm going to make it up to you. Somehow."

"You don't have to do that. The apology was enough." I pause. "I am a little confused about something, though. All during school last year, you teased the crap out of me. It didn't seem like you were that sorry."

"My teasing is playful," he insists, his hands sliding around to my stomach. "I've told you that already."

"Then why did you act like a weirdo when Bradon came up to us while we were talking at your locker?" I decide it's time to be blunt, instead of tiptoeing around everything. Like in London, when I kissed Nyle. I want to be that girl again and stop letting being home get me so down. "Because it felt like you were acting weird, because . . . you were embarrassed to be seen with me." My chest tightens as I think about all the times people were embarrassed to be seen with me. "Which I totally get. I know I'm not even close to being popular or anything, and everyone keeps staring at me like I'm some fungus that crawled out of a swamp."

A strange look crosses his face that I can't decipher. "You think they're staring at you, because they think you're a fungus that crawled out of a swamp?"

"I don't know," I say, puzzled over the odd look he's giving me. "I mean, they probably don't literally think I'm fungus, but they definitely stare at me like I am."

"That's not why they're staring at you. I promise."

"I don't really care why they're gawking. I just want them to stop. It makes me feel self-conscious, and I've had way too much of that in my life. That's what I loved about being overseas. No one knew me, so I never had to worry about people making fun of me."

"No one's making fun of you," he says earnestly. "But I'll see what I can do with the staring."

"What? Are you going to ask the entire school to stop looking at me?" I ask jokingly, expecting him to laugh.

"I could do that, but I think I'll try something else first," he says with a devious smile as he wiggles his brows at me.

"Don't do anything that'll make it worse," I beg, clasping my hands together. "Please, promise me you won't, Kai."

"Cross my heart and hope to die. Stick a needle in Hannah's eye," he says then kisses the tip of my ear before letting me go.

I jolt from the weird kiss move, which only makes him laugh.

"Well, at least you think you're funny," I tease him.

"I *know* you think I'm funny too." He picks up his half eaten apple then flashes me his pearly whites. "It's why you're always laughing when you're around me."

I open my mouth to tease him, to tell him he's never funny, that I never, ever laugh at him, and that he should stop telling jokes all the time, but Kyler walks into the kitchen.

He's wearing loose fitting basketball shorts and a tank top, and his hair is damp, like he just got out of the shower.

The only time I've seen him since I got back from my trip was when he was arguing with Hannah down in the driveway. Being this close to him puts my love/lust meter into confusion mode. I spent three months irritated with him, because I thought he was dating Hannah, and I thought I'd gotten over my crush on him. But then, the other day, I found out he was never really dating her, and now it's left me feeling more confused than ever.

Do I like him still?

Kinda, sorta, yeah.

"Hey, have you seen my gym bag?" Kyler asks Kai as he heads for the fridge. But when he catches sight of me, he freezes, his brows pulling together. "Hey . . ."

"Hey." I wince at the breathiness of my voice.

Get your shit together. Don't be nervous. You're not like that anymore. You kissed Nyle on the London Eye for Christ's sake. And you're not even sure how you feel about him anymore.

Kyler seems to find my spasticness more amusing than repulsive, and smiles at me. I'm convinced he doesn't recognize me, because he's never smiled at me like that before, not even when he gave me the rose or hung out with me while we played basketball.

The rose. The pity gift.

I frown, remembering what Hannah told me. Was there any truth to her words?

"Isa, why do you look like you just ate something sour?" Kai asks, yanking me back to reality.

"Because I did eat something sour," I lie.

Kai rolls his eyes. "Whatever."

"You look different, Isa," Kyler says, studying me from head to toe.

Well, at least he seems to know who I am.

"Um, thanks," I reply, unsure if different is a compliment or not.

"I don't mean that in a bad way," Kyler quickly explains. "I just meant that you look different. Good different, I promise."

He smiles at me, a smile that reaches his eyes. I can't help but smile back and probably look as goofy as Goofy himself.

"Thanks," I tell him with more confidence.

His lips part, but Kai cuts him off.

"Your gym bag's in the car," he says coldly. "You left it there after practice, and Mom blamed it on me. I have no fucking clue why it's my responsibility to take care of your shit."

"She probably thought it was your bag," Kyler tells him, ripping his attention off me. "You always leave yours in there and it stinks up the car."

"I haven't had a gym bag in almost a year." Kai reclines against the counter with his arms folded.

"I thought you were going to try to get back on the team this year?" Kyler asks Kai, using his lean arms to reach up and open one of the top cupboards.

Kai shakes his head with annoyance flaring in his eyes. "That's Mom's wishful thinking. I'm not going to try out for the team. I have better things to do with my time."

"Like what?" Kyler grabs a box of protein bars before shutting the cupboard. "Get high and watch television?"

Okay, things are really starting to get awkward and uncomfortable. I'm deciding whether I should back out of the room and bail, when Kyler turns to me.

"Sorry about that," he says to me. "We shouldn't be arguing like this in front of you."

Kai scowls at Kyler. "Why? She hears us all the time when she's out on her balcony, listening to us."

"Hey." I shoot Kai a dirty look. "Way to throw me under the bus."

Kai looks a tab bit remorseful. "Sorry. But he already knows you do it."

"It's okay," Kyler says to me, tucking the box under his arm. "I always thought it was kind of cute the way you watched us."

He may be trying to make me feel better, but I feel

like a class-A freak right now.

"I have to get to practice." Kyler grabs a bottle of water out of the fridge then backs toward the washroom. "Isa?"

I gradually turn around to look at him. "Yeah?"

"You should come watch one of my games sometime." He flashes me a dimpled grin. "You could come cheer me on and bring me good luck. Like you did with my free shots."

I internally gag. Football. So gross and soooo boring. Seriously, I've been in the room while my dad's watching games, and it's a yawn fest. I'd way rather spend my time reading, drawing, going to Comic-Con, getting my favorite books signed, or blogging. Hell, I'd take running to the paint store in my underwear over watching a bunch of dudes throw a ball around and tackle each other.

But I'm not about to tell Kyler any of this. Not when he just invited me to go see him play. And in public. Not just when we're at one of our houses, where no one can see us.

I plaster on the fakest smile. "Sounds like super fun!" Okay, I might have gone a little overboard with the *super*.

Kyler grins, seeming oblivious to the fact I'm faking my enthusiasm. "Awesome. There's one next Friday. Let me know if you need a ride." He winks at me like Kai does all the time.

I keep on smiling until he leaves the house then my head slumps forward and my mouth falls open. "Holy shit."

Kai snorts a laugh. "Watching you try to sound happy about watching him play was seriously the most entertaining thing I've ever seen."

I sweep loose strands of my rain-kissed hair out of my face then turn to face him. "I hate football, okay. Honestly,

I'm not a fan of watching any sport, period."

"But you play them." He opens the fridge and takes out two cans of Coke. "I remember you winning some sort of free shot contest or something."

"Playing sports and watching them are two totally different things." I catch a can of Coke as he tosses one to me. "I have a short attention span unless it involves books, writing, or drawing."

"I know you do," he says simply while popping the tab of the can open.

"How could you possibly know that about me?" I ask, opening my soda. "No one, except maybe my Grandma, knows that about me."

He thrums his finger against his bottom lip. "Hmmm . . . let me think. How on Earth did I find out all that stuff about you . . . ?" An impish grin plays at his lips. "There has to be some sort of online place where I read all about your interests. Oh yeah, I remember now. There was this page that had all these thoughts of yours on it. There were also some pretty cool pictures of your trip that I didn't see on your phone."

I feel like I've entered the *Twilight Zone*. "You were on my *blog*?!" Shit. Has he read my last entry? If so, then he knows about my mom.

He shrugs, like it's no biggie. "It's kind of interesting, and you're kind of funny."

"Gee, thanks," I say sarcastically. "And you're *kind of* nice."

"Why, thank you," he replies with over exaggerated happiness.

I resist an eye roll then try to get a vibe from him. See if maybe he knows about my mom. Is there pity in his eyes? No, not really. If anything, he appears amused.

"When's the last time you've been on it?" I ask. "My

blog, I mean."

"I don't know, like four or five days ago."

I exhale in relief. I made the post yesterday.

He winds around the kitchen island and heads for the doorway that leads to the living room. "Come on. I need to grab some stuff before I go to the party."

"I never said I was going." It's not like I don't want to go to a party. I just worry that people from my school will be there, which means I'll end up spending the entire night avoiding their stares, probably hiding out in the bathroom.

He spins around, grinning. "Oh, come on. You know you want to go." His grin expands. "It'll be *super* fun!"

I flip him the middle finger, and he laughs.

"Besides, if you go, I can introduce you to some people from our school. Getting to know people is the first step to friendship." He grins.

"You would really do that for me?" I'm oddly touched.

He waves me off, like it's no big deal. "I have excellent people skills. Stick with me and you will too."

Then he grabs my arm and pulls me with him, leaving me no choice but to go.

Chapter
FOURTEEN

"*I have to change before* we leave," I announce to Kai after he walks out of his bedroom, wearing different clothes.

He's now sporting a long-sleeved grey Henley, black jeans, and boots. He also has on a grey knit cap and a collection of leather bands on his wrist, including the one I gave him. I won't ever admit it to him aloud, but he looks dangerously sexy.

He evaluates me from head to toe while shoving up the sleeves of his shirt. "Why? You look fine." He tugs on the bottom of my still-damp tank top. "And I think a lot of people will probably appreciate the wet t-shirt look."

I fold my arms over my chest, mentally cursing myself when my cheeks go all melted chocolate warm.

Please don't notice I'm blushing. Please don't notice I'm blushing.

His lips spread to a grin. "The blush would be an added bonus too. Between the t-shirt and that, you might be able to get free drinks all night."

I square my shoulders, scrounging up the little dignity I have left. "Bradon charges people for drinks at his parties? *Really?*"

"Not all the time, but sometimes." Kai nonchalantly shrugs. "He's an entrepreneur."

I run my hands over the front of my shirt. "As much as I'd love free drinks for the night, I think I'd rather wear some clean, more weather appropriate clothes, and just pay if I drink."

"*If* you drink?" Kai questions with amusement. "You're a virgin drinker, aren't you?"

"Oh, please. You think I spent three months overseas and didn't touch a drink?" I scoff with a roll of my eyes. "I've drank a ton."

His lips twitch as he wrestles back a laugh. "Okay, I believe you. But just a warning, I'd stay away from any baked goods if I were you."

"Warning noted."

I can't believe I'm doing this. Going to a party where I might run into people I know and that Kai is going to introduce me to. This will be so much different, and I'll be way more out of my element, than when I was dancing in clubs and kissing guys I barely knew.

Before Kai and I leave, I go over to my house to change my clothes.

"You can just wait on the sofa, if you want to," I tell him when Kai tags along with me as I head upstairs to my room.

"Nah, I'll just wait outside your bedroom door for you."

"You're such a weirdo."

"That's why we get along so well," he replies, grinning.

Smiling, I dash up the stairs and to my room. After I get the door shut, I head for the closet to pick out an outfit. As I pass by my bed, though, something catches my attention and makes me grind to a halt.

A piece of paper is on the mattress.

I pick it up and my heart slams against my chest. "Holy shit! Holy shit! *Holy shit!*"

Kai bursts into, wide-eyed and panicked. "What happened?"

"I don't . . ." My hands and legs are shaking about as badly as my voice. I sink to the mattress, struggling to catch my breath. "It's nothing. I just found my birth certificate. That's all." When a pucker forms at his brow, I add, "I've been trying to find it for a week or so."

"Okay. I get where all the crazy was coming from now." A beat or two goes by as he glances from me to the paper in my hand then shifts his weight and cracks his knuckles.

"You read my post, didn't you?" I can read the truth all over his face and by how twitchy he's acting. "Why didn't you say anything when we were in your kitchen?" I ask, pushing to my feet. "You said you hadn't read it in like four or five days."

"That was a guesstimate." He seems like he feels guilty. "And I was just saying what I felt like you wanted me to say. It didn't seem like you wanted me to know."

"I didn't. Not yet anyway." Looking down at my birth certificate, my excitement bubble pops, because where the mother's name is supposed to be is blank. But my father's is there in dark ink, a reminder that yes, he may hate me, but I am his flesh and blood.

"So, does it say it?" Kai asks tentatively, leaning over to get a look at the certificate.

I lift my gaze to him. "Say what?"

"Who your mother is. That's why you were so excited to find it, right? Because you want to know who she is."

I really, really wish I would've gone with my gut instinct and deleted that post. "Kai, you can't tell anyone about this, okay? My dad, he doesn't know I'm looking for her, and he got really upset when my grandma asked him about my mom."

"Does Lynn or Hannah know you're looking for her?" His voice conveys worry.

"I don't know." I glance down at the certificate again, and my good mood deflates even more. "Someone had to, though, for this to be sitting on my bed when I walked in." I bite on my lip as I mull it over. "The only person here right now is Hannah."

"You think Hannah put it on your bed?" Kai looks unconvinced.

"Maybe she read my blog," I say, even though the idea is pretty ludicrous.

"I hate to say this, because it might hurt you, but even if she did read your blog, why would Hannah try to help you?"

"Nothing you can say about Hannah is going to hurt me, Kai. I've pretty much developed an immunity to her."

Kai presses his lips together as he stares at me with insinuation in his eyes.

"Why are you looking at me like that?" I ask. "I'm being serious. Hannah doesn't bother me anymore."

"Okay . . . but I've been wondering if maybe your new hot girl look thingy may have had something to do with what I said to you before I left." He stuffs his hands in his pockets, tense as a tightly wound rope. "That this was your way of trying to get her to stop being mean to you all the time."

"That's not what that was about." My tone comes out

more clipped than I want it to, and I clear my throat. "My change was about me. I don't—didn't even know who I was. And I wanted to figure that out."

"You're still kind of confused, it seems like," he accuses, carrying my gaze.

"Maybe a little." *Maybe a lot.* With each passing day, I feel more lost as the possibility of finding my mom grows dimmer.

What if this is it for me? This lonely room with bare walls and a family who loathes me? The idea is so depressing, so dream squashing. *No, I won't go there.*

"You know it's okay, right?" Kai says, scuffing the tip of his boot against the carpet as he stares down at the floor. "To be confused over who you are."

"Are you confused over who you are?" I don't really expect an answer, since he usually changes the subject whenever someone mentions his bad boy makeover.

His gaze elevates to mine and that let-me-hypnotize-you-with-my-eyes look is smoldering fiercely. "I was. It's actually getting clearer now, though," he says then immediately changes the subject. "Quick question, though. Why would Hannah put your certificate on your bed? Isn't that kind of, in a way, helping you find your mom? Because that doesn't seem like something Hannah would do."

"It's not really helping me, since it doesn't have my mom's name listed. I mean, I already know her first name is Bella, but only because my dad let it slip out to my grandma. And he was really mad when he did that." I blow out a stressed breath. "So either this is Hannah's way of rubbing in my face that I'm motherless, or maybe she thinks if she helps me find my mom, it'll get rid of me."

"Now *that* sounds like Hannah." His gaze falls to my

hand and he takes the certificate from me. "Mind if I hang onto this for a couple of days? I may know a guy that could help you with your search. I'm not sure what kind of information he needs, but I could give it a try."

"You know, this is the third time you've said something very mafia-ish to me," I point out. "You want to tell me something about you and these new friends of yours?"

"No way. That would take away all of my mystery." His lips quirk as he looks at me. "Then I'd just be boring Kai again."

"I kind of liked boring Kai." I playfully nudge his foot with mine. "Well, sometimes anyway."

"You never really knew him, Isa. No one really did."

"I did a little, though."

"Maybe a little," he agrees, tucking the certificate into the back pocket of his jeans.

Well, I guess that's that.

It makes me nervous to think about what he's going to do with that piece of paper. Who's this guy he's going to talk to? And how could he find my mom without knowing more than her first name?

"Hurry and get changed and let's hit up this party, so we can relax." He backs toward the door, fishing his phone from his pocket.

Relax? Yeah, fat chance that's going to happen. Now that someone in this house knows what I've been up to for the last week, there's no way I'm ever going to be able to relax again.

Chapter

FIFTEEN

The house where the party is at is way the hell out near the foothills, about a thirty minute or so drive from the suburbs where Kai and I live. For the first half of the drive, Kai and I argue about what song we should listen to. He wants to turn on his party song, which is pretty much just bass and dirty lyrics. When he turns the song on, my ears groan in protest, and I reach forward and snatch up his iPod.

"Hey." Kai blasts me with a zombie rage, 'I'm going to eat your brains out' look. "I know you're new to riding with me, so I'm going to tell you the rules as nicely as I can." He extends his hand over the console to steal the iPod away from me, but misses. "No one, under any circumstances, ever gets to touch my stereo."

Smirking, I line my back against the door so I'm out of his reach then quickly scroll through his songs.

"Isa," he warns, his gaze dancing back and forth between the road and me as he drives down the busy street.

"I'm being serious. I have issues with music."

"Clearly." I snicker as I note some of the songs he has on the device. "Dude, your music taste sucks. What happened to that obsession with 80s punk music? There aren't any songs that are even close to punk."

"I go through music phases." His fingers tighten around the steering wheel as his expression darkens. "And I'm super touchy about people insulting my current music taste." He suddenly relaxes, shaking and rolling out his shoulders. "You know what? I'm going to let that one slide just as long as you put the iPod down."

I quickly tap the folder labeled 'For Your Eyes Only', click the first song, and set the iPod down. A song by Violent Soho flows through the speakers and I smile. "Okay, this one's not too bad."

"Whoa. Whoa. Whoa. You turned on one of my private songs," he says then grins and twists up the volume of the radio, singing along.

Private songs? God, I don't even want to know what he does when he listens to those.

I laugh at my own thoughts and end up doing an awesome snort.

"What's so funny?" Kai asks, giving me a curious, sidelong glance.

I swiftly shake my head. "It's nothing."

A grin creeps up his face. "You were thinking something dirty, weren't you?"

"No, I was just thinking about . . . something."

"About something dirty with my private playlist."

I stick out my tongue at him, and he just laughs. Then I relax back in my seat and cross my legs, moving carefully, since I'm wearing a skirt and don't want to flash him. I matched the skirt with a long-sleeved black shirt, clunky black boots, and a studded leather jacket I bought in one of the shops on Oxford Street in London. I hope I look good enough for a party, but since I've never been to one, I'm unsure.

I run my fingers through my wavy hair, trying to add volume, being careful not to snag any of the braids.

"You look fine," Kai says, misreading my primping.

My hands fall to my lap. "I was just trying to make my hair bounce more."

He taps on the brake to slow for a stoplight then twists in the seat, looking at me with his brow cocked. "Bounce? I didn't know hair bounced."

"Tell that to my cousin Indigo, because she seems to think hair needs to bounce all the time."

"I'll never understand girls sometimes."

"And I'll never understand guys sometimes. It's like one minute, you're sweet, and then the next, you're all like," I drop my voice to a low baritone, "'Whatever, I don't care about anything anymore.'"

"I always care about stuff," he says, driving forward as the light turns green. "Sometimes I just can't show it."

"That's really silly."

"About as silly as pretending we were wizards."

"Hey, I was a witch." I smile as I remember how during our walks home, we'd sometimes stop at the park and pretend we were awesome enough to possess the power of magic. "Not a wizard."

"Whatever. It was still silly. I mean, we were almost thirteen years old for god's sake. We were too old to be playing make-believe." Even though his eyes are glued to the road, I can sense the tension flowing off him.

"Well, I didn't. And I still don't think it's silly." I focus on the shops, the local bank, and the small grocery store lining the street, trying to ignore the pain over how he thinks our time together was silly—that I'm silly.

"You're still the same," he remarks, and I can feel his eyes on me.

"I'm a little different," I reply without looking at him. "But yeah, I'm kind of the same too."

"That's not a bad thing, Isa." His fingers brush right above my injured knee.

I jolt in the seat as his touch ripples across my body and zaps my heart like a defibrillator. *What in the wild, wild, crazyland was that?*

"I know it's not a bad thing. I know I'm weird, but I've always been pretty okay with that. I just wish I knew why." An unsteady breath eases from my lips as I peek down at Kai's hand on my leg and then over to him.

He quickly withdraws his hand and places it on the steering wheel. "Why what?"

"Why I am the way that I am. I've never fit in with anyone, especially my family. And then I found out that Lynn isn't my mom and I kind of, I don't know, felt relieved, which probably makes me a bad person, but that's how I feel."

"That doesn't make you a bad person at all. I've heard some of Hannah's stories, about the stuff they've done to you. You should hate her."

"She's told people about the things she's done to me?" Nausea sets in as I think about all the incriminating pictures she snapped of me doing embarrassing, dorky things. What if she's shown them to everyone?

He offers me a look of empathy. "I'm sorry. I thought you knew."

"No, but I'm not surprised." I scrape at the black nail polish on my fingernails. "Sometimes I wonder if Hannah's always known that we don't have the same mom, and that's why she treats me bad."

"Hannah treats you bad, because she's a spoiled

princess." Kai downshifts the car. "She's basically gotten everything she's wanted since we were kids."

"I know . . . I don't get why people even like her."

"Because they're afraid of her. They'd rather be her friend than her enemy."

"So, you were afraid of her then?" I ask. "Because you liked her once."

"I've never *liked* her." He grinds his teeth. "I told you I just hit on her, because I knew Kyler had a thing for her and it would piss him off. There was never anything more to it."

"If Kyler had a thing for her, then why isn't he dating her anymore?" I attempt not to sound bitter, but fail epically.

"He liked her when he was younger, but grew out of it," he explains, making a right down a side road that weaves between the rolling foothills. "It's probably the one smart thing he's ever done in his life. The whole date thing at the beginning of the summer pretty much happened only because Hannah's pushy as fuck when she wants something."

"I completely agree." I restrain a smile, but it's difficult when I just found out Kyler never really wanted to go out with Hannah. He was probably being nice.

"So, you're still obsessed with him, huh?" Kai asks, jostling me of my Kyler Lust Trance.

"What . . . no . . . I'm not . . ." My cheeks erupt in flames, but fortunately, it's dark enough that there's no way Kai can see my mortification.

"Relax, Isa." He pats my uninjured knee, all buddy, buddy like. "It's not really that big of a secret."

I frown. "But it makes me sound pathetic. Obsessing over some guy for years, who I have no chance in hell of ever going out with."

"Why don't you have a chance?" he asks, genuinely baffled.

"Um, because I'm me."

"Yeah, so? He asked you to his football game, didn't he?"

"I guess he did." I replay the two second conversation I had with Kyler in the kitchen, trying to remember if when he asked me, he was sending out date vibes. But I have zilch experience in the boyfriend department. "You think he was asking me out?"

"Probably." Irritation creeps into his tone. "He's shallow enough that he would."

"Why would him asking me out make him shallow?" I ask, offended.

"Because he doesn't know you, which means he was only asking you out based on the fact that he thinks you're hot now."

"That's kind of harsh. Maybe he knows me and likes me."

"How could he possibly know you?" Kai asks, flipping the blinker. "You two haven't ever talked."

"We hung out a couple of times when I taught him how to improve his free throw shots, and he used to stop Hannah from picking on me," I tell Kai. "There was this one time when he even stopped his own friends from picking on me. A couple of his football buddies had me cornered, because Hannah basically had a choke collar on them. He came up and said something about them being late for practice so they'd have to leave."

"He should have called them out on what they were doing, not just fed them a lame-ass excuse to make them stop without making himself look bad." He makes another turn, this time down a street lined with single-story, seventies-style homes.

"You didn't do that for me either." I clench my hands into fists as they begin to tremble.

I hate memory lane. Let's not go there ever again.

"Yeah, well I was a fucking asshole back then. Still am most of the time, but I don't want to be when I'm around you." He parks the car on a curb at the end of a very long line of vehicles. "My brother, on the other hand, walks around pretending he's all high and mighty, when really, he's a fucking arrogant prick who always puts himself first." He slides the keys out of the ignition. "You may not want to believe this, but you're too sweet and smart for Kyler. It'll never work out." He shoves open the door to get out. "He'd be better off with your sister. The two of them are pretty much the same, except your sister doesn't give a shit that people think she's a douche."

With that, he climbs out of the car, leaving me to wonder if he's right. Could Kyler really be the asshole Kai seems to think he is?

I shake my head. No, there's no way. Not when he's always been so nice to me. Plus, I know he doesn't want to be the guy he is now; like he told me on the porch that day years ago, he wishes he could be different.

I don't care what Kai says. I'm not giving up on my Kyler dream just yet. I want to see where it goes. If it's an epic fail, then at least I'll know, and then I can finally move on.

Chapter
SIXTEEN

I've seen a ton of movies that featured high school parties. I figured the rowdy, loud music and tons of people crammed into a house were Hollywood's played-up versions, but when I catch sight of the single-story home the party is taking place at, I start to think the movies nailed it dead on.

The small living room is jam-packed with a sweaty, unruly, stupidly silly drunk people. Music is booming and vibrates the floors. The smell of sweat, beer, and cigarette smoke laces the air, and I'm pretty sure I just stepped in a puddle that I think might be urine.

"Ew!" I shiver as I stare down at the yellow puddle on the linoleum floor.

I'm distracted just long enough by the grossness that when I look up, I've lost Kai in the crowd. I stand on my tiptoes, panicking as my gaze surfs the crowd. There's just too many people to tell who's who.

"I'm never going to find him." Those old feelings of

ridicule sneak up on me, and I hug my arms around my-self, noting every glance in my direction.

They have to be staring at me. And you want to know why, Isabella? Because they know you don't belong here.

"Hey, I know you, right?" Bradon, Kai's friend, and the guy throwing this shindig, stumbles through the crowd and stops in front of me. He has overly long hair, his eyes are red, and his clothes smell like smoke with a kick. "You're that chick from my school."

I want to point out there's a lot of chicks who go to our school, but I'm guessing I'll probably just confuse him. "Yeah, sure."

"You know Kai, right?" He wags a finger at me. "You're that girl who was by his locker."

Great. I went from being That Chick at School to be-ing That Girl by Kai's Locker.

I stick out my hand to properly introduce myself, so he'll stop giving me lame nicknames. "I'm Isa."

He eyeballs my hand then he wraps his fingers around mine, brings them to his lips, places a kiss on my skin, and then licks me like a dog.

I screech, loud enough to make a scene, and people glance our way. Apparently, drunk people have a short attention span though, because five seconds later, they're all doing their own thing again.

"Sorry, I couldn't help it." He laughs at me as I wipe my hand on the side of my skirt. "I've never had a girl try to shake my hand before."

"If it happens again, you should probably just shake it back," I offer him some advice.

"Thanks. I'll keep that in mind." He noticeably checks me out before peering around the crowd. "So did Kai come with you, or what?"

I inch forward as a guy staggers past me and jabs his

elbow into my back. "Yeah, he did. I don't know where he is, though. I lost him the second I walked in here."

"Yeah, that happens a lot." He looks back at me. "How about I help you find him?"

I nod, my anxiety going down a drop or two. "That sounds great. Thank you."

"No problem." He nods for me to follow him as he pushes his way through the crowd. "We can get you a brownie from the kitchen too." He throws me a toothy smile from over his shoulder. "I make killer fudge brownies. They're actually pretty famous."

"I bet they are," I remark, remembering Kai's warning to stay away from the baked goods. "But I actually don't like brownies that much." *Huh. Never thought that sentence would ever come out of my mouth.*

"That's because you haven't ever tasted mine." He raises his voice as an upbeat song blasts through the speakers and everyone gets all riled up. "One bite will change your mind."

As I get jostled all over the place by the crowd, I thank the heavens that I'm wearing boots; otherwise, I'd be knocked flat on my ass by now. Heels were never my thing, something I learned every time I tried to wear them out to a club. I'd either trip, fall down completely, or my feet would end up hurting so badly that I'd have to sucker Indigo into swapping shoes. The only ones I can tolerate are platforms, but after wearing them to school last week, I've decide they might be as demonic as stilettos.

I struggle to maintain my balance, and Bradon snags my arm and tugs me out of the room, only letting me go when we make it safely to the kitchen. There are a few people hanging around a keg, but other than that, the room's pretty empty.

"Brownie time," Bradon announces as he lifts a paper

towel off a plate. Underneath it are the most gooey and delicious brownies I've ever seen, and my mouth starts to salivate. Bradon picks up the plate and moves it toward me. "Try one. I promise you won't regret it."

I literally have to stab my nails into my palms just to stop myself from snatching one and gobbling it up. "I can't."

"Why not?"

"Well, because . . . they have pot in them, right?"

He chuckles at me. "You're adorable. I can see why Kai likes you."

Before I can even wrap my head around what he said, an arm drops down on my shoulders.

"There you are," Kai says casually, but I can feel the tension in his arm muscles. "I look away for like a second and you disappear on me. What happened?"

"I stepped in piss and got distracted," I explain, glancing down at my boot. "Or at least I think it was piss."

Bradon puts a finger to his lip, seeming way too fixated on me. "Seriously adorable."

Kai gives me a questioning look. "How did you end up with Bradon?"

I lean in, keeping my voice low. "He found me in the crowd, licked my hand when I tried to introduce myself, then brought me in here, offered me a brownie, and called me adorable when I asked him if there was pot in it. I don't know why. I haven't done anything that could remotely constitute being called adorable."

Kai presses his lips together as he angles his head so he can look me in the eye. "You asked him if his brownies had pot in it?" he asks, struggling not to laugh.

"Why is that so amusing?" I feel like the butt of a joke I don't get. "You told me not to eat them, because they have pot in them, right? I just wanted to make sure."

Kai glances at Bradon, who's still staring at me like I've sprouted a unicorn horn out of my forehead.

"Can I borrow her for the night?" Bradon asks Kai, with his bloodshot eyes drinking in my every move.

"I'm not on loan," I quip then shrug. "Sorry."

Kai chokes on a laugh while Bradon blinks at me, confounded.

"Okay, how about we go get you something to drink," Kai says to me then steers me across the kitchen and away from Bradon.

Once we reach the counter lined with all sorts of different shaped alcohol bottles, he lifts his arm from my shoulders. "So, what's your drink?" He holds up his hands. "No, wait a minute. Let me guess. A wine cooler."

"I've never had a wine cooler before," I admit.

He reaches for a bottle filled with red liquid that has tiny little flakes at the bottom, picks it up, pulls a face, and then sets it down. "Then what did you drink while you were overseas?"

"Lots of stuff. Whenever we'd do shots, though, Indigo would always make us do vodka." I shudder, remembering the scorching burn.

Kai muses over something then moves for the fridge. When he returns, he has a beer in his hand. "How about a beer? I don't think it'll make you pull that face you just made when you mentioned vodka."

I gratefully take the beer and twist the cap off while Kai grabs a plastic cup and fixes himself a drink using soda and whiskey.

"Now what do we do?" I ask as he screws the cap back on the whiskey.

"Whatever you want." He downs a large swallow from his cup.

I smile artfully at him. "Okay, well if that's the case

then I want to chase a unicorn, run on a rainbow, and swim in a lake made of gold."

He rolls his eyes at me, but a smile plays at the corners of his lips. "We can do whatever you want within the realm of reality."

"Reality's no fun, though." I pout.

"That's not true," he says, his gaze drifting across the room. "I bet you've had fun in reality before."

"Yeah, I guess." I sip my beer, remembering the time I probably had the most fun. "I did have a lot of fun on my trip."

"Okay, that's a starting point." He swishes around his cup. "What did you do on the trip that was so fun?"

I shrug. "I don't know. I saw a ton of cool stuff and did a crap load of crazy things. You saw the pics on my blog, right?"

"I saw the pics," he says. "But I want to know about these so-called crazy things you did. Because a lot of those photos were of places. Not you."

"We did a lot of stuff, but I guess one of my favorite things was when we went clubbing."

His brows shoot up. "You went clubbing?"

"You don't have to sound so shocked about it." I chug down half my beer as my social anxiety jumps onstage and takes me over like a puppet. I know it's insane, but it feels like his surprise screams, '*You don't belong here!*'

"I'm sorry," he tells me sincerely. "You just threw me off. I mean, the Isa I knew didn't dance."

"Well, she can dance now." I straighten my shoulders as the beer swims through my veins. "And let me tell you, she's *awesome*."

"Is that so?" he remarks, rubbing his jawline.

I cringe, seeing where he's heading with this. "Yeah, but only when I'm in clubs."

He nods his head at the living room where people are packed together like sardines, grinding together like they've been drinking liquid hormones. "This place is kind of club-ish."

"Not really." I fight back the panic strangling my throat. "Kai, please don't make me dance in front of all these people. I know some of them."

"It'll be fine. I'll even dance with you." He guzzles down a huge mouthful of his drink, tosses the cup into the garbage, threads his fingers through mine, and then hauls me toward the living room.

Before we dive head-on into the dancing orgy, Kai lets go of me and walks over to the stereo system in the corner of the room. Bradon is sitting near it, sipping on a drink. When Kai approaches him and says something, Bradon makes a face and promptly shakes his head.

"No way!" Bradon shouts, standing to his feet and placing himself in front of the stereo. "That'll never happen, dude."

"Oh, come on!" Kai begs, reaching for the stereo. "Just let me do it."

Bradon swats his hand away. "You know I don't take request like that unless it's from a hot chick."

Kai throws a quick glance at me then leans in and says something to Bradon. I don't know what he's saying, but I have a feeling he might be using me to get his song request past Bradon.

Bradon frowns but reclines back over the table and presses a few buttons before he sits up. The room grows quiet and people immediately start complaining.

"Turn the fucking music on!" A lanky guy not too far away from me hollers.

"Bradon, quit begin a dick!" a girl wearing a flowing floral dress shouts, red-faced and pissed as hell.

"You owe me, dude," Bradon grumbles as Kai struts back toward me.

He gives him a thumbs up without turning around, walking right for me. "All right, it's dancing time," he says, rubbing his hands together.

"What'd you get him to turn on?" I ask, but then a song clicks on and I have my answer. I giggle. "You picked a Katy Perry song?"

"What? She rocks!" he replies, owning his song choice. He snatches hold of my hand and drags me through the people who've started dancing again. "Now come on. You owe me a dance."

"How do you figure I owe you a dance?" I stumble after him as he shoves his way to the center of the room.

He elbows people out of the way to clear some space then his fingertips press down on my wrist and he spins me around so my back is aligned with his chest. "Because you never gave me the wand you promised me."

I start to laugh, then stop myself. "You never gave me a chance to give you the wand. Three days after I promised you I'd make you one, you decided you were too cool to walk home with me anymore."

"I came to your house after that happened," he says. "You could've given it to me then."

I tip my chin up to look at him. "When did you come to my house?"

"After I told my friend you were stalking me." Remorse fills his eyes. "I wanted to say sorry. I know it wouldn't have meant much, since I wasn't planning on telling people the truth, but I felt bad."

"Why didn't I know that you stopped by my house?"

"Probably because Hannah answered the door and I chickened out."

The mention of Hannah painfully reminds me of the

birth certificate and how she put it on my bed for me to find. If she's trying to get rid of me then that's probably the tip of the iceberg. Who knows what other kinds of mean games are waiting for me at home?

"Stop overthinking and dance." He grinds his hips against my backside and I laugh, finding it funnier than I probably should.

But this is Kai, not some random stranger at a club who Indigo roped into dancing with me. Kai, who used to walk home with me, who secretly shared my love for magic, superheroes, and zombies. Who teases me constantly and who pisses me off sometimes.

He seems pretty adamant about dancing with me, though, upping his moves as he grips my hips and pulls me closer.

"Okay, I guess we're doing this then." I down the rest of my beer, knowing I'm going to need it, then set the empty beer bottle down on the floor.

Giving one final panicked glance at the people around me, I sway my hips and rock to the beat of the music. I don't move slowly either. That's not my style. I may have social anxiety, but give me a drink and some loud music, and I'll go wild. I'm talking freak out, lose your mind, whip it, shake your groove thang kind of dancing. I blame it on Indigo and the first time we went out clubbing.

Kai's hand slides around to my stomach, his fingers dipping under the hem of my shirt. When his knuckles graze my bare skin right above my hipbone, I have a hard time focusing. And breathing. Suddenly, I no longer think dancing with him is that funny. I find it. . . . well, sexy.

His fingers trace circles on my skin as he grinds his hips against me. I fight to keep moving the way I was before all the touching started, but I keep spacing out and forgetting how to function.

His breath caresses my ear as he chuckles. "You seem tense. I thought you said you could dance."

He's so doing this on purpose. To distract me.

"Yep, I sure can," I say, and then really start dancing, ignoring everything around me like I did when I was overseas.

I lift my arms, sway my hips, and rock out, matching the beat of the song. Kai lines his body up with mine and we move together perfectly. Song after song, we keep going, practically having sex with our clothes on. I'd be embarrassed—and maybe I will be, come morning—but right now, I'm having fun.

I'm not sure how long we dance or how long it would've gone on, but then Kai ruins the moment by licking the side of my neck.

I squeal, whirling toward him while I wipe his slobber off my neck.

He gives me an innocent look. "What? That's how I thought all the cool kids were greeting each other tonight."

I keep my hand cupped over the side of my neck for protection. "First of all, you weren't trying to greet me. And second of all, it creeped the hell out of me when Bradon licked me."

His chest shakes as he fights not to laugh at me. "I don't think I'm as creepy as Bradon."

"You know what? You're right." Which means I can pay him back. I let my arm fall to the side, lean forward, and lick his neck like a dog.

He jumps back, startled, and then busts up laughing, hunching over as he grasps his side. Unable to help myself, I join in with him.

After the laughter dies down, we mutually agree not to lick each other anymore and start dancing again. By the time we stop to get some water, we're sweaty, hot, and out of breath. We wander back to the kitchen and Kai gets a bottle of water from the fridge, taking a sip before handing it to me. I down most of the water in just a few gulps then hand the bottle back to him.

"Now you've got me curious," Kai says after he finishes the rest of the water.

"Over what?" I ask, wiping my damp forehead with my hand.

"Who taught you how to dance like that?"

"That awesomeness can't be taught. It's just pure talent."

Chuckling, he fixes himself another drink, this time mostly whiskey and a splash of soda. "All right, you own your awesomeness."

I smile as he hands me a beer. I open the bottle then trail after him as he glides the sliding glass door open and ducks outside onto the back patio. The crisp night air feels great on my sweaty skin as I step outside. I figure the reason why Kai came out here was to get some fresh air, but he continues down the steps and heads toward a pool house in the far back corner of the yard.

Unsure if he wants me to follow him, I lollygag on the patio, keeping my distance from a couple of guys lounging in the lawn chairs, smoking and laughing about something.

"You coming? Or are you just going to stand there?" Kai hollers when he stops in front of the pool house door, the porch light hitting his face.

Relieved he isn't making me stand there by myself, I hurry down the stairs and across the grass to him, gulping down my beer.

"I wasn't sure if you wanted me to follow you or not," I say, picking at the label on the beer bottle.

"Silly girl, of course I wanted you to follow me," he replies, his speech starting to slur.

I laugh at him. "You're so drunk."

"No way," he insists, stumbling and bumping his elbow on the door. He blinks as he looks inside his cup. "Okay, maybe just a little." He sets his cup down on a rusty patio table, raises his hand, and taps his knuckles against the door.

"What are we doing out here?" I put the mouth of the bottle to my lips and take another drink.

A drunkenly droopy grin spreads across his face that makes him so adorably cute it's ridiculous. "This is my connection." He pats the door like it's his best friend.

I lower the bottle from my mouth. "Connection?"

He pats the back pocket of his jeans where my birth certificate is tucked away. "This is where my guy is."

I stare at the rotting wooden door. "Your guy lives in Bradon's pool house?"

"No, he just chills here a lot."

"Um, okay."

"It's not as sketchy as it sounds."

"Good. Because it sounds pretty damn sketchy."

"I would never let anything happen to you." He drapes his arm around my shoulders and I get a whiff of his whiskey breath. "Remember the cave?"

It takes me a moment or two to sort through my beer-laced thoughts and figure out what he's talking about. Back when we hung out, we found this hollowed out tree that we nicknamed 'the cave', where nothing bad could ever happen to us.

"When I'm in the cave, my sister Hannah and my mom can't see me," I said as I slid inside the hollow trunk. "And maybe my dad can."

"When I'm in the cave, I get to be me," Kai said as he

ducked in behind me. "No one else, including my mom or dad, can try to make me be anyone else."

"And we have to promise never to tell anyone about this place." I hugged my knees to my chest to make room for his gangly legs.

He bent awkwardly until he fit inside. "It's a deal."

"Cross your heart." I traced an X across my heart. "Hope to die. Stick a needle in Hannah's eye."

He laughed at me and sketched an X across his chest. "I promise."

"I wonder if the tree's still there," I say with a trace of a smile.

"It is," Kai assures me, averting his gaze from mine.

"How do you know?"

"Because I sometimes go there to think."

"Really? That's . . . kind of nice, I guess."

He shrugs, staring at the ground. "You should also know that I sometimes get high there too."

I crinkle my nose. "So you do get high?"

"Not for a while, but yeah, if we're totally being honest, I did it a handful of times over the summer."

"But you seemed so irritated over people accusing you of doing drugs."

"I was irritated." His jaw clenches. "I know it's not an excuse, but I was going through some shit, and it was the only way to clear my head."

"Are you still going through some shit?" I blame the beer for asking the question.

His lips part to answer, but the door swings open, and relief washes over his face as he turns away from me.

"Kai, what's up, man?" A large guy wearing a backwards baseball cap, netted shorts, and a stained white shirt stands in the doorway with his fist extended toward Kai.

Kai bumps knuckles with him. "Not much. Just came to see what's been going on."

"Not a whole fucking lot," the guy replies, leaning against the doorway. "Business has been super fucking slow."

"That sucks, man," Kai says. "But I might have a little bit of business for you."

"Really?" The guy rubs his goatee. "What kind of business are we talking about?"

Kai glances at me from the corner of his eye and the guy tracks his gaze. Even with the beer in my system, I still squirm as he scrutinizes me.

"Who's your friend?" he asks Kai, giving a chin nod in my direction.

I shyly wave back.

"This is Isa." Kai drags his hand over his head, tugging off his knitted cap. He ruffles his fingers through his hair, causing the strands to go askew. "She's actually the one who's in need of your ever-so-awesome services."

"Is that so?" he asks thoughtfully.

I smile warily, unsure what to say. Kai hasn't even told me who this guy is or what his services are, and it feels like I have a bundle of crazed-out monkeys inside my tummy.

"She cool?" he asks Kai, straightening his stance.

"Yep. I'll even vouch for her," Kai says, crossing his arms.

Okay, I don't care what he says. Kai is *so* in the mafia.

The guy mulls it over a second or two then sticks out his hand toward me. "Isa, I'm Big Doug."

"It's nice to meet you, Big Doug." I take his hand and shake it, hoping he doesn't lick me like Bradon did.

"My pleasure. My pleasure." His hand dwarfs mine as he gives it a soft squeeze. Then he pulls away, moves back, and motions for us to come inside. "Welcome to my paradise."

Big Doug's paradise consists of four brick walls, a floor cluttered with boxes, old candy wrappers, and soda cans, and a table covered in computer screens, wires, modems, and all sorts of electronic stuff I know I've never seen before.

"Are you a hacker or something?" I don't mean to say it aloud, and I slap my hand over my mouth, worried I've crossed a line.

Luckily, Big Doug seems fine with it. "Hacking's just one of my talents." He waddles over to the table, kicking trash out of the way. Facing us, he sits down on the edge of the table. "But the question is . . . what talent do you want? Because I got a lot. All cost money, of course. I take cash or credit, depending on how well I know you."

My gaze slides to Kai and he shrugs, like *what*? I want to ask him so many questions, starting with how he knows a hacker, but I'm not about to ask in front of Big Doug.

"Just put it on my tab." Kai places a hand on the small of my back, trying to reassure me. "You know I'm good for it."

Tab? Huh?

"Oh, okay. I didn't realize this was your thing." Big Doug stares at me just long enough to make me squirm then he fastens his attention on Kai. "So what's the job?"

Kai retrieves my birth certificate from his pocket and hands it over, giving Big Doug a quick explanation of what's been going on.

"I was hoping you could take a look at the certificate and see if it's a fake or not," Kai says when he's finished explaining about my mom. "And if it is, I was hoping you'd have a couple of ideas on how to track her mom down."

Big Doug fiddles with the corner of the certificate. "All you know is her name's Bella?" he asks, and Kai nods. "And your father's name is Henry Anders, right?" This time, he directs his question at me.

I nod, crossing my fingers he'll do this. This may be illegal, but it still seems way less terrifying than asking my dad.

"I have one question before I agree to do this," Big Doug says to me. "Why not just ask your dad who she is?"

"Because he doesn't want me to know who she is, for some reason," I explain. "I didn't even know about her up until a few months ago."

"Are you even sure she's alive?" he asks, setting the certificate down on the table beside one of the computers.

I shake my head, folding my arm around my stomach as my gut twists into knots. "I don't know anything other than I lived with her for the first few years of my life before I went to live with my dad . . . and her name is Bella."

He bobs his head up and down. "Okay, give me a couple of weeks, and I'll see what I can come up with."

"Thanks, man," Kai says, sticking out his fist again.

The two of them bump knuckles again then Kai and I head out the door. I don't say anything else until we've reached the back patio. The guys that were there earlier have abandoned the lawn chairs and the entire area is quiet.

"Okay, what the hell was that?" I spin to face Kai, spreading my arms out to the side.

"What do you 'mean what the hell was that'?" Kai stares up at the stars. "That was me helping you out."

"That was some sketchy stuff. And how do you even

know Big Doug?"

"I met him through Bradon. Did a little work for him a while back." He's still transfixed by the stars, so I pinch his arm to get him to look at me. "Ow." He chuckles, meeting my gaze as he laughs. "What was that for?"

"I just want to know that you're not going to get into trouble for that," I say, putting my hands on my hips.

"Why would I get in trouble? Big Doug's the one doing all the work." He reaches forward and slips his fingers through mine, moving my hand away from my hip. "Now let's go inside and celebrate."

"Celebrate what?" I stare at our interlaced hands, confused over why he keeps touching me and why I feel comfortable with it.

"That in a week, you'll know who your mom is." He pulls me toward the door.

I let him steer me back inside, crossing my fingers that he's right and that Big Doug will be able to find my mom.

But what I really hope is that she'll be alive when I do find her.

Chapter
SEVENTEEN

Two shots and a beer later, I'm headed outside to wait for Indigo to come pick mine and Kai's sorry drunk asses up.

"You feeling better about going to school now?" Kai asks me as we reach the curb.

He spent the last three hours introducing me to everyone. While I don't have anyone I'd call my best friend, I do feel better about going to school. And no one brought up the mental institution thing, so I'm guessing they've all forgotten about that rumor.

"Yeah, thanks for introducing me to so many people," I say through a yawn.

"I feel bad I didn't do it sooner," he says.

"I don't blame you. It's not like I'm the kind of person everyone wants to get to know. I'm too weird, and hardly anyone gets me."

"Isa, you're ridiculously freakin' awesome. Everyone who gets to know you is lucky."

"You're sweet when you're drunk," I tease with a nudge of my elbow.

"I'm always sweet when I'm around you, baby." He giggles.

I giggle too. "You're a cheesy drunk." I yawn again and lean against Kai, my eyelids feeling heavy. "I shouldn't have drank so much."

"Just focus on that firefly over there." He points across the street at a glowing light. "It makes it easier to keep your eyes open."

I giggle again. "Kai, that's not a firefly. That's a porch light."

He leans all of his weight against me, nearly making me topple to the ground. "Hold me up, or I'm going to fall."

"You're a guy," I whine, digging my feet into the ground to support his weight. "You're supposed to hold me up."

"That's very sexist of you, Isa." He tsks, waving his finger at me. "I'm so disappointed."

I shake my head, but a smile tickles at my lips. "Jesus, you're a handful."

"I know." He sighs tiredly. "If only I were like Kyler, then life would be so much easier for me and everyone around me."

My muscles ravel into knots as I stiffen, sensing a drunken talk coming. You know the kind, where you yammer and pour your heart out with someone then when you sober up you have an oh-God-what-have-I-done moment.

"Kai, you're a good guy, no matter what you think."

"Yeah, tell that to my parents. Or my grandparents. Everyone in the entire Meyers family."

"Parents can suck, but that doesn't mean you have to

believe everything they try to stick in your head. You're free to think whatever you want about yourself. Trust me."

"You wouldn't be saying that if you knew everything I did. I'm not a good person. I've done so much fucked up stuff."

"Everyone's done fucked up stuff," I say, shutting my eyes. I wonder what he's done. Why he thinks he's so bad. "It doesn't make you a bad person. You just need to forgive yourself."

"Easier said than done." He yawns, sinking to the ground and clumsily pulling me with him.

I trip over his feet and his fingers delve into my skin as he tries to stop me from falling. But we end up going down hard and landing in the grass in a tangle of legs and arms.

"Kai, you're the clumsiest drunk ever!" I laugh, trying to push him off me.

"Don't lie. I'm the funniest drunk ever." He laughs . . . well, more like drunkenly giggles, as he rolls off me and onto his back. "And you're the cutest drunk ever."

"I so am not." I lie down with him so our heads, arms, and legs are touching. I look up at the stars twinkling in the sky, like handfuls of magic pixie dust. "And you wouldn't be saying that if you saw some of the stuff I did when I was in Scotland."

"Enlighten me then." He tucks his arm under his head then looks at me.

"No way." I keep my eyes on the stars.

"Come on, just one tiny thing, and then I'll let it go."

"Yeah, right. I'm learning you're the kind of person who doesn't just let things go."

"That does kind of sound like me," he agrees then

reaches over and tickles my side.

"Kai!" I erupt in a fit of giggles. "Stop with the tickling!"

"No way." His hands travel downward to the bottom of my shirt and his sneaky little fingers dip under the fabric. He tickles me on my bare stomach, which feels ten times worse, yet somehow ten times better. "It's too much fun watching you laugh."

"You're evil!"

"I know. You're the hero and I'm the villain, right?"

"Yep! But you'll never win." I flip onto my stomach, ungracefully push to my feet, and skitter away from him.

He stands up too, although it takes him a few attempts to get his feet under him. Then he moves for me with his hands up, but grinds to a halt as a group of older guys stroll across the grass toward us.

"Hey, Kai, how's it going, man?" one guy asks, and not in a friendly kind of way.

Kai tenses by my side. "T, what's up? I didn't know you were going to be here."

"Of course I'd be here. There's no way I was going to miss a chance to pay a visit to my friend." He says *friend* like it's a foul word.

I squint through the dark, trying to see what the guy looks like, but I've got my drunk beer goggles on.

"Who's this?" T asks Kai, smiling in my direction.

Kai grabs my arm and pulls me behind him. "What do you want?"

"I just wanted to pay you a visit," T says. "Make sure you haven't forgotten the deal."

"I haven't," Kai replies through gritted teeth.

Before anyone can say anything else, a car stops in the middle of the road and beeps the horn several times. I'm so relieved to see her. Not just because I missed her, but because this T guy is giving me the heebie-jeebies.

"That's Indigo." I grab Kai's hand before I step off the curb, mostly because I'm worried he's going to fall.

"I'll be in touch," T calls out to Kai as I open the back door of the car.

"Who was that?" I ask as I help Kai get into the backseat.

"Just some dude who thinks he's the shit," he says tightly.

I know there's more to the story, but now's not the time to press him, especially with T still watching us.

I shut the door and slide into the passenger seat.

"Having fun?" Indigo asks with an insinuating smirk. She has on her pajamas, her hair is braided back, and she's wearing her square-framed reading glasses.

I buckle my seatbelt and tell Kai to put on his. "It was just a party. No biggie."

"Sure it wasn't." Indigo shifts the car and drives forward, glancing in the rearview mirror at the backseat. "So you're Kai, huh?"

Kai, who seems to have gotten a second burst of energy, scoots forward in the seat and rests his arms on the console. "Yep, the one and only. But the question is how did you know that?" He eyes her over suspiciously.

"Isa told me about you," she says, pulling out onto the main road. "And I saw some of your texts you sent her while we were on our trip."

As his gaze glides to me, he props his elbow onto the console and rests his chin on his hand. "You've been telling people about me, huh?"

"Don't get too excited. I just told her about my annoying next door neighbor; that's all." I blast Indigo with a warning look, silently begging her to keep quiet.

"I'm not lying for you." She laughs as she reaches for

the knob on the stereo. "So don't look at me like that."

A lazy grin expands across Kai's face. "So what have you been saying about me? I want to know."

"I'm sure you do." I slip off my boots and prop my feet onto the dash, wiggling my toes.

He sticks out his bottom lip and flutters his eyelashes at me. "Pretty please?"

I shake my head. "No way."

"Oh, come on." He pouts. "Most girls fall for that look all the time."

"Ah-ha! I knew you did that look on purpose to try to get your way." I point at him. "But it's not going to work on me, because I'm not like most girls."

"I know you're not." He turns dead serious. "And that's such a good thing. Seriously. We should hang out all the time. It's just too much fun with you."

"Isa, he's totally adorable." Indigo practically swoons in her seat.

"Hey, what a freakishly awesome coincidence," Kai says, sitting up straight. "My friend calls you adorable. Yours calls me adorable. We should be adorable together."

"Aw," Indigo says, pressing her hand to her heart.

"Don't *aw* anything he says," I tell her. "He doesn't even know what he's saying. He's too drunk."

"I am not." But his eyelids start to drift shut, validating my point.

"I don't care if he's drunk or not. He's a cutie, Isa." She slows down for a stop sign and twists the stereo knob, surfing through the stations.

I peek back at Kai, who's dozing off, his head tipped back, and he's making this funny bubbling noise with his lips. He looks like a goof, but . . ."Okay, he's a little bit cute, but in a goofy way."

"So are you." She smiles at me. "But that's why I love

you."

Kai suddenly wakes up, bounces forward, and slams his hand against the console. "Holy crap. Turn this shit up!"

Indigo leaves the radio on the station and cranks up the volume. A pop song I'm vaguely familiar with flows through the speakers and the bass booms. Kai and Indigo start singing, bobbing their heads, and shimmying their shoulders.

"Well, at least you two share the same taste in bad music!" I laugh, because they look ridiculous, and I love them for it.

"Isa's kind of a music snob," Kai remarks between lyrics.

"Don't let her fool you," Indigo says then belts out more lyrics as she drives through the intersection. "She knows this song." She reaches over and pinches my side. "Come on, Isa, sing it." When I shake my head, she pinches me again. "Do it. Do it."

Kai chants with her until finally I throw up my hands, surrendering. "Fine! But only because I can't take the peer pressure."

The three of us sing and dance together, creating a sound that kind of resembles a herd of dying cats. By the time the song is finished, Kai is passed out in the backseat.

"I'm really glad you called me tonight," Indigo says as she steers the car through the sleepy town of Sunnyvale and toward my subdivision.

"I promised you I'd never drink and drive or get into a car with someone who has been drinking," I say, resting my head back against the seat.

"That's not the only reason I'm glad." She flips the blinker on and changes lanes. "I tried to call you tonight. I have something I need to tell you."

I take out my phone from my pocket. "The battery's dead." I tuck the phone away then rotate in the seat. "What's up?"

"I found this box while I was going through some of Grandma Stephy's old stuff," she says as she pulls into my driveway. All the lights in the house are off, which hopefully means Hannah isn't home. "There was a box with your dad's name on it, and I think I found something you might want." After she pushes the shifter into park, she opens the console, takes out a crinkled photo, and hands it to me.

The picture is of a woman holding a little girl, probably around two or three, and they're smiling at something in the distance. They have the same blue eyes and brown hair, looking similar enough that they could be mother and daughter.

"Who is this? Wait. You think . . ." I blink at Indigo. "You think this is my mom and me?"

"I'm not sure, but I wonder if it might be. I don't even think your dad knows the photo was in the box. It was rolled up and stuck inside the bottom of a lamp. I actually thought it was a joint at first, but then I pulled it out and . . ." She trails off, staring at the closed garage door. "It was so weird how it was put in there, almost like someone hid it in there."

"Maybe my dad did it," I say quietly. "Maybe he wanted to keep something of my mother, but he didn't want Lynn to know about it."

"Maybe. Or maybe your mom put it in there for you to find it."

"That sounds like a huge stretch. And how would my mom even get a lamp into a box of my dad's old stuff? It doesn't make any sense."

Her gaze glides to me. "I asked Grandma Stephy why

the box was there and she said it your dad asked her to store it for her."

"Which means he probably put it there." I look down at the photo and swallow hard. We look so happy together. Happy. God, I want to feel it again, how I felt in this photo. "Maybe he's still in love with her, and that's why he hid it."

"But that doesn't explain why he won't tell you about her," she points out. "Or why you lived with her for three years before she gave you up."

My lungs ache as I struggle to get air. "Maybe that's because she died. Maybe he took me in because she died, and he keeps this photo because he wants to hold onto her memory."

"That's deep, Isa." She thrums her fingernails on top of the wheel, frowning. "Maybe a little too deep for your dad."

"Who knows how deep my dad is?" Tears prickle in the corners of my eyes. "I don't know him."

"No one really does when you think about it. He's practically secluded himself from the entire family."

She's right. No one really knows my dad, except for maybe Lynn, who practically controls his every move. I wonder if at one time my mom knew him, though. Like really knew him. Were they happy? How did they end up together? Did she make him laugh? Did he make her smile? Was he the one who took the picture? Did the three of us ever spend time together?

All questions I may never get the answers to.

I smash my lips together as I stare at the photo.

Who are you? Where did you go?

How do I find you?

I tuck the photo into my pocket, say goodbye to Indigo, and then climb out of the car. Kai doesn't get out right away, so I open the back door and give him a little shake. His eyelashes flutter open and he blinks at me, disoriented.

"We're home," I tell him softly.

He sticks out his hand and wiggles his fingers. "Help me up."

I grab his hand and tug on his arm. He slides to the edge of the seat and ducks out, bumping his head on the way.

"Ow." He rubs his head, frowning. "The sad thing is I didn't even feel it."

"Then why'd you say ow for?" I tease him as I give Indigo another wave and close the door.

She backs away, her headlights vanishing as she turns onto the road.

"Because it seemed necessary," Kai replies, belatedly answering my question. He hikes down the driveway, weaving back and forth.

Concerned he's not going to make it, I hurry after him as he heads for the sidewalk. But right at the last second, he skips to the side and bounds over the fence, clipping his boot on the top bar. His knees bang the fence and he lands on the other side on his back.

"Shit." I rush over to him and swing my leg over the fence.

I must be drunker than I thought, because climbing over is a lot more complicated than it should be. But I manage without falling then rush to Kai's side, kneeling in the grass beside him.

His eyes are closed and he's lying still with his arm draped over his stomach.

"Are you okay?" I ask, and panic when he doesn't respond. I lean over him and cup his scruffy cheek, trying to remember if he hit his head. "Kai, can you hear me?"

"No, I think you need to lean a little bit closer," he whispers. Then his eyes pop open and a lazy half grin spreads across his face. "Hey."

"Hey." I exhale, relaxing. "You scared me."

"It was just a little fall."

"Did you hit your head?"

"I don't think so." His nose twitches as strands of my hair tickle his face. "Your hair smells good. Like cookies."

"I'm surprised it doesn't smell like beer and sweat." I start to move back, but he combs his fingers through my hair and draws me closer.

"No, don't go," he whispers, his fingers finding my cheek.

I realize a second too late what he wants to do, and the lag in my thought process gives his lips just enough time to reach mine.

I gasp against his mouth as he urges my lips apart with his tongue. Warmth pulls through my veins, steals the air from my lungs, and sends explosions of heat through my body.

Holy hell almighty. So that's what kissing is about?

But right as I kiss him back, headlights shine across us as a car pulls into the driveway.

I trip to my feet and scoot back from him as reality sets in. *Oh. My. God. I just kissed Kai.*

Kai sighs, pushing onto his elbows. "Well, this is going to suck."

At first, I think he's referring to the kiss, but as he gets to his feet, he mutters, "Isa, I'm so sorry you have to see this." Then he places himself in front of me, as if he's protecting me from something.

Before I can ask, the headlights turn off. I peek over my shoulder as I hear the doors slam. The only light around is from a few street and porch lights, and the moon shining in the sky above us. I can barely make out his parents' silhouettes, but I can feel the tension in the air.

"What the hell are you doing out here?" Kai's dad asks as he stares Kai down with his arms crossed.

"I just got back from somewhere," Kai says, sounding so unsure of himself, so unlike the Kai I know.

"Do you realize how late it is?" his mother asks. "No, I don't even want to hear you try to lie your way out of this. Of course you know how late it is. But just like always, you don't care if you worry us."

"You were looking for me?" Kai asks, surprised.

"No. We were at an event," his mother replies curtly. "But what if we had been looking for you? Imagine how worried we would've been."

"Yeah, I don't think you would've been that concerned." Kai yawns and then shakes his head, getting sleepy again.

"Are you drunk?" His mother huffs, tapping her foot against the concrete.

Kai doesn't even try to lie his way out of it. "I'm sorry."

"Dammit, Kai. How many times have I told you if you're going to act like a loser then don't come home," his dad snaps. "Why do you have to be such a fuck-up? Kyler never put us through this shit. Why can't you be more like him, instead of such a fucking loser all the time? Why don't you try making our lives simple, instead of so damn hard all the time? Fuck!" His dad kicks the tire.

"Because then we wouldn't get to have these little chats of ours," Kai mumbles under his breath.

"Get your damn ass in the house," his dad growls as he points to the door. "Right now, before I make you."

Sighing, Kai gives me a little push back toward the

fence before he walks toward the house with his shoulders hunched. I slink into the shadows, wondering what will happen if they see me. Luckily, they seem too distracted by Kai. His dad scolds him the entire way to the back steps then slaps him upside the back of his head as they disappear inside.

Poor Kai. I feel so bad for him. He sounded so beaten down, like he'd heard the speech a million times. It reminds me so much of the way I react to situations, so I know how terrible he's probably feeling right now. I want to go knock on the door and give him a hug, but know it'll probably just upset his parents more.

I make a promise to myself that even if things are awkward tomorrow, which I'm guessing after the kiss they will be, that I'll give him that hug or something.

Chapter
EIGHTEEN

I drank more than I thought at the party, and end up spending almost the entire next day in bed. I keep having the same dream, where someone sneaks into my room while I'm sleeping and stares down at me in my bed, holding a paintbrush. Around six o'clock or so, I wake up and realize where the dream came from. The second I open my eyes and fully come out of dreamland, my nostrils are assaulted by paint fumes. I sit up, look around for where the smell is coming from, and then smile.

A partially finished mural is painted on the wall opposite my bed. The colors are bright and form a city, yet the shadows and fine lines give it a darker, gothic vibe. Standing in front of the industrial scene is a girl who resembles one of my superheroes in my sketches. She's wearing a cape with has her hands on her hips and a look in her eyes that reads: *I'm about to kick your ass.*

I roll out of bed, grab my leather jacket from the floor, and dig out my phone. I have one new message, and without even thinking, I open it.

> *T: U better pay up soon or u r going to get fucked up.*
> *Don't make me remind u what we did to DG.*

I reread the message again then realize I have Kai's phone. I pick up my jacket again and fumble through my pockets until I find my phone. They look almost identical, but I have no clue how I ended up with both.

I set his phone on the nightstand and plug mine in, since the battery is dead. What I read in Kai's message haunts my thoughts as my phone boots up. Who's this T person? And why are they threatening Kai? And what the hell did they do to this DG guy? It has me really worried about him and what he's done to piss off people who are sketchy enough to threaten him.

Once I get my phone on, I plant my ass down on my bed and send Indigo a message.

> *Me: I can't believe u did all of that while I was sleeping.*
> *It's beautiful. Thanks so much!*

> *Indigo: U R welcome! After last night, I thought u*
> *could use some cheering up.*

> *Me: I totally could :) U r the best.*

> *Indigo: I know. And FYI, u sleep like a rock. Seriously, I*
> *thought the fumes would wake u up, but nope.*

> *Me: I was really hungover.*

> *Indigo: I figured as much. Speaking of hangovers, how's*
> *your cute friend doing?*

> *Me: I'm guessing u mean Kai.*

> *Indigo: He's such a sweetie, Isa. Screw this Kyler dude.*
> *U should totally b going out with him.*

Me: U haven't even met Kyler, so how can u say that?

Indigo: I don't have to meet Kyler. The way u and Kai were together was enough.

Me: I'm not going for either brother.

Indigo: Liar. U still have your sights set on Kyler. I can tell.

Me: He did ask me to go to his game yesterday.

I get hyped up and excited just thinking about it.

Indigo: Holy shit! Why didn't u text me?

Me: I got sidetracked with Kai and the party, but I was gonna tell u.

Indigo: Got distracted with Kai and the party. Interesting . . .

Me: And on that note, I have to go.

Indigo: Liar! U r just running from the truth about u and Kai!

Me: There's no truth to me and Kai, because there's no me and Kai. We r just FRIENDS!

Indigo: That's how all true loves start.

Me: TTYL, matchmaker. I have to go take care of some stuff.

I put down my phone, feeling flustered over all the stuff she said. Kai may be cute and charming—and yeah, we shared that drunken kiss last night that made my body tingle in ways I don't understand—but I've never thought of him in the way Indigo was implying until she implied it. Now my mind is all overloaded with thoughts of me and Kai doing more than just kissing. It makes me really confused about myself, what I want, and what the hell I'm doing.

"Dammit, Indigo." I climb out of bed, grab a black shirt, a white skirt, and my gladiator sandals, and then head to the bathroom to take a shower and hopefully clear my mind.

By the time I'm all showered and cleaned up, I feel much better. But as I make it downstairs, my good mood goes *kerplunk*.

Hannah is in the kitchen, and she's not alone. With her are Val, one of her friends from high school, and a beefy guy I've never met before.

"Oh look, it's Isabella Smellera," Hannah sneers as she slams the fridge door.

Val giggles as she collects a plastic cup from off the countertop. "Nice one, Hannah."

"You know that nickname doesn't bother me anymore," I say to her quietly as I cross the kitchen and head for the backdoor.

"Keep telling yourself that." Hannah removes the plastic off a vegetable tray and opens a cup of ranch dip.

I note all the alcohol bottles on the kitchen table and the shiny pink shoes and glittery black dress she's wearing. "Are you having a party?"

"Yep. Sure am. And you're not invited." Hannah readjusts her boobs, and Beefy Dude grins as he watches. "So you better find someplace else to sleep."

"You can't kick me out of my own house," I say, grabbing the doorknob.

"I can't, huh? How about I just text Mom and Dad and find out how they feel?" She laughs snidely when I remain silent. "Yeah, that's what I thought. So get your shit and get out of here."

I fight every damn urge in my body to go back and ninja kick the crap out of her.

"Oh and Isa?" Hannah says, and I grind my teeth until my jaw hurts. "Did you find the present I left for you on your bed?"

I want to ask her why she gave it to me, what her motive was, but that'd be asking for more taunting and ridicule, so I shut my eyes and suck in a huge breath of air. *Don't let her get to you. Just walk away, Isa.* I yank open the door and step outside, her laughter hitting my back.

I shove all thoughts of Hannah aside as I head over to the Meyers' to return Kai's phone to him. As I hike up the driveway, Indigo's texts ring through my head and nerves bubble in my stomach.

"You don't like Kai like that," I mutter to myself as I march up the porch stairs to the backdoor. "You're just friends. You're just friends." I knock on the door, and when it swings open, Kyler stands in the doorway.

He's wearing dark jeans and a red t-shirt that brings out the color in his eyes. His hair is all crazy, like he's been stressed out and pulling on the roots. He looks so sexy right now that I can't stop ogling him.

"Hey, Isa." He places his hand on his head and flattens down the crazy hair.

Hearing him say my name makes my heart thud deafeningly inside my chest, and blood roars in my eardrums at the sight of him.

"Is Kai here?" I want to jump up and down that my voice came out steady.

"You actually just missed him." He braces his palms on the doorframe and I try not to gawk at his flexed arm muscles. "What'd you need him for? Maybe I can help."

My fingers tremble slightly as I stuff my hand into my

jacket pocket and grab Kai's phone. "I'm not sure how it happened, but somehow during the mass confusion that was last night, I ended up with his phone."

He takes the phone from me, his forehead creasing. "You guys hung out last night?"

"Yeah, we went to a party one of his friends had." *And then kissed in the driveway, but he doesn't need to know that.*

He glances up from the phone and at me, his confusion deepening. "You went to one of his friends' parties?" he asks and I nod, puzzled, because . . . well, he's puzzled. "Isa, I don't want you to take this the wrong way, but I don't think you should be hanging out with Kai's friends. They'll get you into trouble."

I don't know whether I'm touched that he's looking out for me or annoyed that he thinks I'm too naïve to take care of myself. "It was just one party. I don't really hang out with them."

"Okay, it's just that . . ." He massages the back of his neck. "You've never really hung out with Kai up until recently, so I just wanted to warn you that he hasn't been making the best choices lately."

"Thanks for the warning." I start back down the stairs, surprisingly relieved to be getting away from the uncomfortable conversation.

"Hey, what are you doing for the next couple of hours?" he asks before I can make my escape.

I stop on the bottom stair and turn around. "I was actually going to head home and blog for a little while. Then I probably have to find a way to get over to my grandma's so I can crash there for the night."

"How come you need a place to crash?" he asks, glancing over at my house.

"Hannah's having a party, and I'm not allowed there

while she has one." I shrug, wondering if he's going to act all offish now because I brought up Hannah.

He pats the doorframe a couple of times. "If you want to wait for me to get done baking, I can give you a ride."

"Really?" Tap dances and fist pumps all around. "That'd actually be super great." *Face-palm. Seriously? What the hell is with all the 'supers' every time I'm around him?*

He motions for me to come inside as he steps back into the washroom.

I jog up the stairs, squeeze by him into the house, and take a whiff of the air. "What are you baking?"

He shuts the door then moves past me and into the kitchen. "Chocolate chip cookies." When I start to grin, he adds, "Don't get too excited. I've never done this before, so I'm not sure how they're going to turn out." He stops in front of the island that's covered with bowls, spoons, eggshells, and layers of flour. "Maybe you could help me out. I know how much you like sweet stuff. Every time you came over here, you always ate all the cookies."

I'm surprised he remembers that about me.

"I don't think I'll be any help," I tell him apologetically. "I like to eat them, but I suck at baking."

He picks up a spoon and looks over a page of a cookbook. "I'm sure the two of us can figure it out, if we put our heads together."

"Okay, we can try that." I stand beside him anyway. I recollect all the times Lynn baked cookies and how she did it, but since she never let me help her when I asked, I lack great knowledge on cooking. "Where are you at in the recipe?"

"I'm not sure." He licks batter off the spoon and then gags. "God, that's disgusting."

"That's because you basically just ate eggs and flour."

I peer into one of the mixing bowls then cover my mouth, trying not to laugh at the bubbling goo inside.

"Is it that bad?" he asks, setting the spoon down.

I shake my head, but laughter is choking me to death. "I'm sorry. I know I shouldn't be laughing."

"No, you really should." He laughs with me. "This is such a disaster."

I get my laughter under control. "Why are you even trying to bake?"

"It's for my mom. She does this fundraiser bake sale every year for the school, and she always takes on too much, so I usually help her out." He pulls a face at the mess on the counter. "Usually she supervises, though."

"Disaster or not, it was really nice of you to try."

"Yeah, I just hope she has time to fix the mess." He picks up the bowl and puts it into the sink, giving up.

I get an idea right as he starts to clean up. "I might know someone who can help us."

"Really?" He perks up as he turns on the sink to rinse the bowl out. "Who?"

"My grandma. She's not the greatest cook, but she can make a mean batch of cookies."

"You think she'd help us?"

"I can text her and find out." I slide my phone out of my pocket. "I need to tell her I'm spending the night there anyway."

"Thanks, Isa." His mouth tips to an adorable half-grin. "That's really awesome of you."

"It's not a big deal." I'm such a liar. It's such a big deal to me that my hands shake as I text Grandma Stephy.

> Me: Hey, can I stay the night there? Hannah kicked me out.

"It is a big deal," Kyler insists. "You're always so nice

and always willing to help people, even when they haven't treated you as nicely as they should."

My brows furrow. "Are you talking about you?"

He nods, cleaning a glob of yolk off the counter with a paper towel. "I haven't always treated you as nicely as I should. I never even thanked you for making my free shot skills awesome."

I shrug. "Like I said, it's not—"

"Don't say it isn't a big deal," he cuts me off. "I've been thinking about this a lot lately, mainly when things with your sister went south, and I realized I can come off as an arrogant dick sometimes."

"Why did things going south with my sister make you realize that?" I don't know why I ask, but I have this overwhelming urge to know.

"I kissed her," he says almost guiltily. "And I never should have kissed her, because I didn't like her that way. But the fact of the matter was I kissed her and she took it the wrong way, and it made me feel like such a douche. And then I started thinking about how many times I acted like a douche, and it started to drive me crazy."

"Hannah's ego can take it. I promise."

"I know." He steadily carries my gaze. "But there's other people who might—who shouldn't have to put up with my shit."

I shrug. "You never really did anything to me. And you've always stuck up for me when other people were acting like douches."

"Yeah, I guess." He tosses the paper towel into the trash and then scratches his forehead. "You know, you're so easy to talk to. I don't know how, but I somehow forgot you were like that."

"You know, you're not the only guy who's told me that."

"Really?" He seems intrigued. "I guess I'll have to think of a better compliment then."

"I guess you will." The light, flirty tone of my voice shocks the crap out of me, and I honestly kind of feel silly for even attempting to flirt. Fortunately, my phone buzzes. "Hold on a sec," I tell Kyler. "My grandma just texted me back."

Grandma Stephy: Goddamn that child. She's such a pain in the ass. Of course u can stay, but does your father know about this? Because he's been really upset with me lately.

Me: Maybe we should just keep this between us. If I text him about Hannah kicking me out, it's just going to start more drama, and there's way too much of that already.

Grandma Stephy: Okay, sweetie. I'll come pick u up.

Me: I actually have a ride, but I need to ask u for another favor. I have a friend who has a cooking crisis and needs help baking a few batches of chocolate chip cookies. I love eating me some cookies, but u know I suck at actually making them, so I thought maybe u could help us out.

Grandma Stephy: So u want me to cook for u? Jesus, aren't u needy ;)

Me: I know. It's your fault, though, for giving me everything I want ;)

Grandma Stephy: Glad to c u haven't lost your sense of humor.

Me: That'll never happen, no matter how bad things get.

Grandma Stephy: You're a strong girl, Isa. U really r. And I love u to death. I'll cook for u, but only if u tell me who this friend is.

Me: Um . . . Kyler Meyers, a guy who lives next door to me.

Grandma Stephy: Is that the boy u and Indigo were always whispering about?

Me: Maybe

Grandma Stephy: Interesting.

Me: Please don't say anything weird while we're there.

Grandma Stephy: I'll try my best, but no promises.

"So what'd she say?" Kyler asks. "Will she help us out?"

I glance from the screen and find him standing in front of me, close enough I can smell his cologne. "She said she's down."

"Really? That's so fucking awesome. Thanks, Isa." He hugs me. Actually freaking hugs me, with both arms and everything. "I owe you big time. And not just for the cookies, but for teaching me how to kick ass at free shots."

"I am pretty awesome," I joke, daring to wrap an arm around him and hug him back.

"You're more than awesome. You're like the awesom-est of awesomeness."

I smile at his sentence, because it sounds like something I would say.

"Okay, who died?" Kai says, sounding like he's right next to us.

"Huh?" Kyler pulls away from me and his gaze cuts to his brother. "What are you talking about? No one died."

He might be wrong, because I'm pretty sure my heart stopped beating for a second or two there.

Kai gives me a condemning look as he drops his jacket onto the table. "I don't know. Isa might have."

My lips do a great Elvis impression as Kai and I stare each other down. Surprisingly, Kai is the one to give in first and whisks by me to grab a package of Oreos from the cupboard.

"Well, it looks like you two are having a fan-fucking-tastic time," Kai says dryly to Kyler and me. "I'll leave you guys to your awkward hugging."

"I actually came here to bring you your phone," I call out after him as he turns to leave the room. "I somehow ended up with it last night."

He turns around, facing me again. "I was wondering where that went. I was worried I lost it at Bradon's and he'd already hocked it." I notice a red mark on the side of his cheek and wonder if it's from where his dad slapped him upside the head last night.

You need to make sure everything's okay.

"He sounds like a great friend," Kyler says sarcastically as he puts the eggs back into the fridge.

"Yep, the best," Kai quips, peeling apart an Oreo to lick off the frosting. Then he fixes his eyes on me. "Did you bring my phone with you? I've been expecting a few texts."

Kyler chucks it at him before I can answer.

Luckily, Kai has the reflexes of a ninja and he effortlessly catches it. "Thanks." He smiles at Kyler, but it's not a friendly smile. "Have fun with your new friend, Isa." He winks at me, trying to get under my skin, then turns to leave, scrolling through his messages.

I hurry after him as he walks toward the stairway. "Who's this T guy?"

He glances down at me, not looking very happy. "You know who he is. He's that dude who talked to us last night."

"But who is he exactly?"

"Just some dude."

"Don't lie to me, Kai. I read one of your messages from him." I shift my weight as he glares at me. "It wasn't on purpose. I thought it was my phone."

"You should probably just forget what you read." He punches a few buttons then stuffs it into the back pocket of his worn jeans.

"Are you in trouble?" I ask. "Because that message . . . it sounded like you were in trouble."

"I'm always in trouble," he replies simply then stuffs a cookie into his mouth and licks his lips.

His tongue.

Those lips.

That kiss.

"Kai, about last night and what happened in the driveway—"

"Relax." He cuts me off. "I kiss almost everyone when I'm drunk."

"I wasn't actually going to say anything about the kiss, but thanks for the info on your kissing routine," I say, and he stares at me, unimpressed. "I just want to make sure you're okay . . . with what happened with your dad." I suck in an inhale, mustering up the courage. "And to give you this." I wrap my arms around him and give him a quick hug that lasts just long enough for me to notice he smells like vanilla frosting. "You looked like you needed this last night, but I didn't want to make your parents madder, so I thought I'd wait until today."

The hug is not as awkward as I thought it would be, but when I step back, Kai's staring at me with his mouth hanging open.

"You're a strange girl sometimes." He grabs another cookie from the package with a quizzical look on his face. "But in the best way possible."

"So I've been told," I say with a small smile. "You're okay, though, right?"

He nods, swallowing hard. "I'm okay."

I glance at the welt on his cheek. "Promise?"

His fingers drift to his cheek and he winces. "I promise."

Then he turns his back on me and jogs up the stairs without saying anything else.

I'm not positive I believe he's okay, but I'm not sure what else to do, other than keep an eye on him.

I head back to the kitchen, feeling sullen.

Kyler has gotten everything cleaned up by the time I walk in, and has his jacket and shoes on, ready to go.

"Everything okay?" he asks as he collects the car keys from the counter.

I nod. "Yeah, everything's fine."

That's the second time I've lied in the last ten minutes. But who I'm lying to, I'm not quite sure.

Chapter
NINETEEN

By the time we arrive at my Grandma Stephy's house, she's halfway done with baking the cookies. I give her a good, stern lecture for not waiting for us, but she tells me that she doesn't need my sucky cooking skills tainting her cookies and to go sit my ass down in the living room while she works her Baker Fairy Magic in the kitchen.

"She's funny," Kyler says after we settle on the living room sofa.

"Yeah, she's pretty funny, I guess." I shift on the sofa, feeling nervous as hell with how close he's sitting next to me.

"You smile around her a lot," he remarks as he slides his arm across the back of the chair.

"Do I not smile a lot when I'm not around her?" *Do you notice that I don't?*

"I've seen you smile a couple of times," he says. "But not a lot."

"Maybe it's because you haven't been around me a

lot," I reply with a shrug. "Generally, I try to be a happy person, even when things are super sucky. And I'm seriously easy to please. I mean, give me a cookie and a comic book, and I'm like a freaking unicorn sniffing rainbows."

"A unicorn sniffing a rainbow?" He cocks a brow.

I shrug, picking at my nails. "What? Unicorns are totally crazy happy when they sniff rainbows."

He chuckles. "Funny. I didn't know unicorns were real or that they sniffed rainbows."

"Oh, they're totally real," I joke with a grin. "Now, I'm not positive the rainbow part is true, but I like to think it is, because I'm just that awesome."

"That you are." He gently tugs on a strand of my hair for God knows what reason. "You remember that time you wore a cape to school?"

I pull a face. "Yeah, I remember. Don't judge me, though. I was like ten and going through this phase where I wanted to be a witch."

"No, I wasn't judging you at all," he quickly says. "I always thought it was cool you were so comfortable with being yourself." I glance down at my stylish outfit and he hurriedly adds, "I like this look too. I promise. And you're still you and everything. And really cool and comfortable with yourself." He's rambling and nervous, and I can barely keep up with what he's saying. He finally takes a breath and shakes his head at himself. "I don't know what my problem is. You've totally thrown me off my game."

He's trying to use his game on me?

He moves his arm from the back of the sofa and rakes his fingers through his hair. "You just make me nervous."

I almost bust up laughing. *I'm* making Kyler nervous? "Are you being serious?"

He nods, lowering his hand to his lap. "I'm usually

better at reading people, but with you . . . I have no idea what you're thinking." He waits, like he expects me to tell him.

I shake my head. "There is no way I'm telling you what goes on in here." I tap my temple with my finger. "If I did, then you might run out the door."

"I doubt that." He sits up straight and twists to face me. "But how about we try it and see? You tell me one thing you're thinking, and we'll see if it scares me enough that I run."

"That seems like a game I'll lose no matter what, because either you leave, or you stay here and think I'm crazy."

"Okay, well how about this? You just tell me one thing, and I won't think you're crazy and I'll stay."

"How can you possibly predict that?" I ask amusedly. "Are you secretly a psychic?"

"I have an aunt who is," he says in all seriousness.

"Really? That's crazy cool. Does she, like, tell you your fortunes and everything? Do you know when you're going to die?"

He shakes his head. "Nope. I'm not telling you anything more until you tell me something about you."

I give an overdramatic sigh. "Fine, but don't say I didn't warn you." I press my lips together, thinking, *What could I possibly tell him about me that won't make him think I'm crazy?* All my interests are weird, and I don't think he'd get my obsession with zombies. Maybe I could tell him some of the things I did this summer, like dancing at the club or kissing Nyle . . .

Oh, my God, why would I tell him that? "I skinny-dipped in a pool this summer." I slap my hand over my mouth. Holy shit. Out of all the things, that's what I decided to go with?

"You did what?" From the kitchen, Grandma Stephy stares at me in shock.

"We weren't totally naked," I tell her, mentally cursing myself. I'd been doing so well, lightly flirting, saying fun things, and then my weirdo gene decided to make a grand appearance.

She points the spoon she's holding at me. "We'll talk about this later." She goes back to her cooking, leaving me to sit here in shame as I blush.

"You really did that?" Kyler asks, trying not to smile.

"I didn't mean to say that aloud. I do stuff like that sometimes. Talk without thinking." I lean back in the sofa. "But yeah, Indigo—my cousin—and I went swimming in our underwear when we were in Scotland. It was more her idea than mine. She was really big on making sure we had a ton of crazy experiences."

"It sounds like that's exactly what you did." He playfully bumps knees with mine. "Maybe one day you could tell me more crazy stuff you did."

I bite back a smile. "Maybe one day, if you're lucky."

He grins, totally noting my flirty tone. "Maybe when you come watch my game, we can go out and get something to eat. Hit up a party or something."

Okay, he's definitely asking me out. I get all giddy, but then I hesitate. I don't know why, but at that moment, I think about Kai and the party we went to. We had so much fun. More fun than I've ever had. Would I have that much fun with Kyler? I'll never know unless I go. Besides, going out with Kyler has been my dream since practically forever. I owe it to my eight-year-old self to do this. And talking with him today has been so easy.

"That sounds like fun," I say. "And I think it has crazy adventure potential."

"I think so too." He glances at his watch. "You'll have

to be the leader of our little adventure. I'm not very good at impulsive things."

"I'll think of something," I promise him as he glances at his watch again. Am I boring him to death?

"I still can't believe you went to Scotland," he says, staring at me in awe. "I mean, I knew you went some-where for the summer, but not Scotland."

I wonder where he thought I was this summer. Did he buy into Hannah's mental institution thing? "Where ex-actly did you think I went this summer? I'm just curious."

"I knew you went on a trip with your grandma, but Kai never said exactly where you went." He pauses, seeming conflicted. "Were you worried about Hannah's rumor and the mental institution thing? Because, you should know, no one believes that."

"Really?" I hug a pillow against my chest. "Why not?"

"Kai told everyone that it wasn't true." He intently studies my expression. "You didn't know that?"

"No, I didn't. He never said anything to me about it." My thoughts drift to Kai.

Why didn't he tell me? I wish I knew, so I could at least thank him.

God, I need to thank him, like a lot.

"Okay, I'm new at this not-being-a-douche thing, so you can totally tell me if I'm being rude," he says with a hint of remorse in his voice. "But the games on in, like, five minutes and I—"

I laugh, cutting him off. "Kyler, you can turn on the game. It's cool."

"Are you sure?"

"Yep." I'm just glad I know what all the watch-check-ing was about.

I turn on the television for him and his attention

instantly goes right to the screen. I think about sending Kai a text and thanking him, but a text doesn't feel like the right way.

No, it should be in person.

Eventually, the air laces with the scent of soon-to-be done, yummy-in-my-tummy cookies. I've just started contemplating getting up and going into the kitchen, wondering if it makes me rude, when Kyler turns to me.

"You want me to explain the rules to you?" Kyler asks as a commercial comes on. "If you're going to come watch me play, you should probably know what's going on. That way you can cheer me on when I kick some ass." He winks at me. "I kick ass a lot."

"I bet you do," I tell him, smiling from the wink. "You can try to explain the rules to me, but I'm going to warn you that I usually don't catch on to stuff very quickly, unless I'm actually doing it."

"I guess we'll have to throw the ball around sometime then." The dimple grin appears and my pulse quickens. "But I'll try to explain it now, if that's cool." He gets an excited look in his eyes, like he's pumped to be doing this.

The look is contagious and gets me pumped too, even if we're going to be talking about football.

He faces the television again, sitting back in the chair and putting his arm on the back again. "Okay, so how much do you know about football?"

"A little bit." I'm hyperaware that he's playing with my hair. I don't even think he realizes he's doing it. "My dad watches it sometimes, but he's not a fan of me being anywhere near him when he does."

"But you're good at sports, right?"

"I'm okay, I guess. But football's always seemed kind of boring to me." I offer him an apologetic look. "Sorry."

"It's okay. I'm not one of those guys who thinks the game is everything. You don't have to like it. But I want to try to get you to kind of maybe like it enough not to be bored out of your mind when you're at my game, okay?" he asks and I nod.

He smiles and jumps right in, yammering about downs, defense and offense, goals, two point conversions. By the time he slows down, my mind is on football overdrive.

"It's okay if you don't get it all at first," he says when he notes the crazed, wild-eye look I'm probably rocking.

"Good, because I'm definitely not getting it at all." I look at the television screen. "I mean, I get the gist of it, but there's so many rules and so many guys just running around on a field."

"I'm probably boring you to death, aren't I?" He shifts positions, sitting up straight and lowering his hand to his lap. "I have an idea. How about for every rule I tell you, you get to tell me one thing about comics and superheroes."

"You know I'm into that stuff?"

He nods. "I've seen some of your drawings at school too. They're pretty good."

I mull over his offer. "All right, Kyler, you have yourself a deal."

An hour later, he's leaving with his freshly baked cookies and his head crammed full of superpower knowledge. I feel like I'm floating on clouds and skipping on rainbows, even if my head aches from football facts.

The second the door closes, I overdramatically fall to the floor. "What the hell just happened?" I say, draping my arm over my head. "Did I seriously just spend over an hour talking to Kyler about football and Jedi mind skills?"

Grandma Stephy laughs at me as she starts piling dirty bowls into the sink. "To be young and in love again. I've completely forgotten how silly love can make someone."

"I'm not in love with Kyler. I'm just . . ." I push up on my elbows. "You did hear him, right? I mean, I didn't dream what just happened, did I? Because I've dreamt about him asking me out for a long, long time." Well, up until recently. Lately, my dreams have been chock full of worries about never finding my mom.

"You're awake. I promise." She grabs a dishtowel and tosses it at my face. "Now, get your ass over here and help me clean up this mess."

I drag myself off the floor and put the flour and sugar into the pantry. "Can I ask you a question?"

"Isabella Anders, you need to stop asking that question before you ask a question," she gripes as she puts the egg carton back into the fridge.

"Sorry, but I kind of wanted to prepare you for what I was about to ask."

She pauses, worry creasing her face. "What is it?"

I sigh then tell her about the photo and the birth certificate, omitting the details of what Kai and I did with the certificate.

"I thought I told you to leave this alone and let me handle this. That snooping around wasn't a good idea," she says when I'm finished.

"I can't just sit around and wonder what's going on." I pull out a barstool and sit down. "It's driving me crazy not knowing what happened, where she is, who she is. I feel like I don't know who I am anymore. Like I'm just this person floating around in the world, lost, without a family. And I don't want to float anymore."

She takes a seat on a barstool beside me. "Honey, I know it's confusing right now, but give me some time to get the story out of your father. I know it's not happening as fast as you like, but I really do believe that eventually he'll break down and tell us if I push him just enough."

I glance down at my bandaged knee, remembering the last time she tried to push him. "You really think you'll be able to get him to tell you?"

She hesitantly nods. "Eventually, yes."

I want to believe her—I really do—but I've heard the two of them yelling on the phone at each other over the last couple of weeks, and my dad seems pretty dead set on no one telling me anything about my mom.

"Do you have that photo on you?" she asks, wiping her hands off on a dishtowel.

I retrieve the picture from my pocket and hand it to her.

A faint smile rises on her lips. "You look a lot like her."

"Have you ever seen her before?"

She shakes her head. "I'm sorry. I really am. I wish you didn't have to go through this."

"It's not your fault." I suck back the tears, get up, and start sweeping the kitchen floor.

But one question is stuck in my head. How did my dad manage to keep my mom such a secret?

"Isa, stop sweeping. The last thing you should be doing is cleaning." She stands up and grabs her purse from the table. "Why don't we go out for dinner? We can go to that diner you love, and I'll even let you order dessert first."

"That sounds nice." I smile so she'll relax, but deep

down, I know that even sugar isn't going to cure the hole forming in the center of my heart.

The only thing that will ever fix it is finding my real mom.

Chapter

TWENTY

Shit has officially hit the fan. Because Sunday morning, when I return home from my grandma's, Lynn is there. And she's alone.

"Where's Dad?" I ask as I enter the kitchen, which is still trashed from Hannah's party she had last night.

"He had to make a quick trip out to Florida for work," she answers, sorting through the stack of mail on the counter littered with beer cans and plastic cups.

My muscles ravel into knots as I remember how shitty she treated me the last time my dad went on a business trip. "How long will he be gone?"

"A week or so." She sets the mail down and gives me a look that sends a chill down my spine. "And I'm under strict orders to make sure you do your chores while he's gone."

"My room and bathroom are already clean," I say, hoping Hannah's friends didn't trash those rooms too.

"That's nice, but I was talking about your new, extra

chores." Her smile grows as her gaze sweeps around the kitchen.

"But I didn't make this mess," I say, fighting to keep calm, because losing my cool is only going to make this worse. "I wasn't even here."

"How do I know that for sure, though?" She grabs the handle of her suitcase and drags it with her as she heads for the doorway. "It makes much more sense to me that you would have the party. Hannah's too good of a girl. Now hurry and get this place cleaned, so I can give you your list of chores."

I grip the edge of the counter and bite back a stream of expletives clawing up my throat.

This is going to be a hellishly long week.

For the next week and a half I play the role of Isabella Smellera, cleaning and taking on the role as the maid for my mom and Hannah. I thought my dad would be back by now, but every time I ask Lynn about when he's coming home, she just shrugs and says, "He'll be back when he gets back. Now get to work."

I try to call my dad a couple of times, but my calls go straight to voicemail. I try text and email, but I receive no reply. By the time Friday rolls around, it's been two weeks since I've seen or heard from my father, and I'm beginning to get really concerned that maybe Lynn murdered him on their getaway and dropped his body into the ocean.

"I'm sure he's fine," Kai says as I express my concern to him during third period. "I know Lynn's a bitch and everything, but I don't think she'd kill anyone." He flashes me a teasing grin, trying to lighten the mood. "It'd be too messy for her, and she wouldn't risk getting blood on her clothes."

"I hope you're right." I add shading to the drawing I'm working on, instead of doing the math assignment.

Kai and I haven't really hung out very much lately, mostly because I've been too busy cleaning the house and cooking for Lynn and Hannah. Same with me and Kyler, but we do have a date scheduled for tomorrow. Now, whether I can get out of the house to actually go on it is an entirely different question.

As for Kai and his issues with his parents, I haven't had a chance to ask him more about that, but I haven't noticed any more welts on him or heard any yelling next door. That doesn't mean I'm going to stop keeping an eye on him.

And the kiss . . . well, somehow the two of us have silently agreed never to mention it again. I think about it sometimes, though. Just like I think about Kyler.

I'm a very, very confused girl.

"I'm always right," Kai jokes, reaching across the row to flick my hair with a pencil. "You should know that by now."

"Kai and Isa, keep it down," Mr. Marelli warns from his desk.

Half the class turns and stares at us. While the staring has toned down, I still haven't made any real friends. I do have a few people I chat with during classes, thanks to Kai and that party, where he introduced me to people.

Kai rolls his eyes, but faces forward in his desk again, and starts scribbling the answers on the assignment sheet. I work on my sketch again, getting lost as I draw the superhero version of me.

"You need a sidekick," Kai whispers, leaning over in his chair to look at my work.

"I usually have one," I whisper back as I draw an angled line. "But I thought I'd go solo on this mission."

"No way. I want to come." He does his pouty lip, fluttery eyelash move. "Come on. Make me your sidekick."

Grinning, I press the pencil to the paper and give into his request.

He smiles, relaxing back in his chair with his arms tucked behind his head. "See? The move does work on you."

My grin grows as I finish the drawing then hold it up for him to see.

"Why does my head look so big?" he wonders, putting the tip of the pencil to his lip.

"It has to be big," I explain, "in order to fit your superhero name."

"Which is?"

"Ego Man."

"Isa, come on," he whines. "I know you can do better than that."

"I don't know. Ego Man seems pretty fitting."

"Fine, but if I'm Ego Man, then you're Vain Girl, and our kryptonite is mirrors, because we stare in them for too long."

I giggle softly. "I'm not vain."

"And I don't have an inflated ego," he insists. "But hey, you're the one who wanted to play this game."

"A game I'm winning." I show him my pearly whites.

He rolls his eyes. "In your dreams."

"Isa and Kai, this is your final warning," Mr. Marelli warns, scowling at us.

We both grow quiet until Kai says, "But then what happens to us? I mean, his threat seemed so ominous, but he didn't finish it."

I choke on a laugh and Kai grins. Unfortunately for

us, Mr. Marelli doesn't think it's so funny and makes Kai move to the desk at the front of the classroom. I spend the rest of class working on the assignment and dreading lunch, since I still spend it sitting alone in the cafeteria.

When the bell rings, I slowly put my stuff away to kill time.

"What are you doing for lunch?" Kai asks as he strolls down the aisle toward my desk.

"What I always do." I swing my backpack over my shoulder. "Go to the cafeteria and eat lunch."

"Ew, you eat in the cafeteria?" He pulls an I'm-gonna-barf face.

"It's the only place to eat, since I don't have a car to drive anywhere."

"I don't have my car today either. I had to let Kyler borrow it, because his is in the shop." He frowns as if just realizing this.

"You can always eat with me," I offer. "In the ewy cafeteria."

His expression contorts with disgust. "There's no way I'm eating that food." He looks at the clock and then at the door. "Come on. I have an idea."

I follow him out into the busy hallway, where he finds a girl named Marla, who I think's a junior and who has a car. Using his eyelash fluttering move, he sweet talks her into giving us a ride to Sunnyvale Burger Drive-In, although she doesn't seem too thrilled I'm included in the 'us'.

I spend most of the drive in the backseat, listening to her laugh at everything Kai says, even stuff that's not funny at all. When we reach the burger place, Kai thanks her for the ride then hops out and opens the door for me.

"Wait? You don't need a ride back to school?" she asks, leaning over the console and smiling at him as her cleavage pops out of her top. "Because I don't mind giving you one."

"We're actually going to walk somewhere after we get our food." Kai shuts the door after I climb out.

The hope in her eyes goes *poof,* and I kind of feel bad for her. "Okay, well if you ever need a ride again, just let me know." With that, she glares at me before pushing the shifter into reverse and backing out of the space.

"I think I'm cramping your style," I tell Kai as we head for the entrance doors. "Did you see that dirty look she gave me?"

Kai feigns dumb. "I didn't notice anything."

"You liar." I pinch his ribs.

He laughs as he opens the door and lets me walk through first. "You're so violent all the time."

"Just admit it," I say as I walk up to the counter. "You totally just played her."

"I told her straight up that we needed a ride." He examines the menu above the register. "She knew the plan the entire time—that I was going to get lunch with you. She let herself get played."

I decide to let it go, because I'm dying to ask something else. "Why are you eating lunch with me? You never have before."

"Usually I have stuff to do at lunch." He keeps his attention fixed on the menu. "But since I don't have a car today, that stuff's been put on hold until tomorrow."

"What kind of stuff?"

"Just stuff."

Ever since I read the text from T, I've been really worried about him. I keep waiting for him to show up at school with bruises or broken bones, but so far, he seems okay. Still, I have to wonder what exactly he owes this T guy that would lead to such threats.

"But you're okay, right?"

"I'm always okay," he says without looking at me.

I don't think I believe him.

After we get our lunch, we leave the burger place and start down the sidewalk, and not in the direction of our school.

"Where are we going?" I ask then sip on the straw of my shake.

He winks at me as he pops a fry into his mouth. "It's a surprise."

I pull my aviator sunglasses down over my eyes to block out the blinding sunlight. "We won't be late for class, though, right?"

"We might be a few minutes late." He puts his own sunglasses on. "But I promise it'll be worth it."

He picks up his pace and I chase after him as he makes a right and ducks into the park. The moment he jogs to the grassy area, I know where he's going and it makes me grin like a goof.

I race after him as he sprints toward the hollowed out tree tucked away near the rickety old seesaw. When we reach it, Kai ducks in and I follow. But since we're taller than we used to be, getting us both in becomes a puzzle. We end up sitting side by side with our legs sticking out of the entrance.

"I miss coming here," I state as I peel the wrapper off my hamburger. "It's so quiet and peaceful."

"I'm actually surprised they haven't cut the tree down yet," he says, pulling his burger out of the bag. "They've cut down a ton of them already."

I pick off the pickles and take a bite of my burger. "Maybe this one's still here, because they know it's magical."

Kai chuckles at me as he chews his food. "Maybe, but

I doubt it."

"You never know." I steal a fry from him and pop it into my mouth. "It could be magical."

His expression tightens. "I don't believe in magic anymore, so I can't agree with you."

The edge in his tone makes my concern for his well-being go up about fifty thousand notches.

"Kai, I know you don't want to talk about it—you've made that pretty clear—but just promise me you're going to be okay. That the threat that T guy made to you won't really happen."

He stares out the hole, chewing on his food. "I'll be okay."

"Promise?"

He looks at me, his eyes smoldering. "Isa, you don't need to worry about me. I can take care of myself."

"I know I don't *need* to worry about you," I say, sounding a little worked up. "But I do."

"Why?" he wonders, still keeping his intense stare fixed on me.

I swallow hard. "Because I just do." I haven't thanked him yet for telling everyone that Hannah's rumor was false, and it feels like the right time. "Kai, I want to thank you."

"Oh yeah? For what?" He seems really distracted.

"For telling everyone I didn't spend a summer in a mental institution."

"You found out about that?"

I nod. "I've been meaning to thank you, but I wanted to make sure it was when we were alone so I could press how much it means to me. No one's ever done something like that for me, especially when I was such a dork."

"It's not a big deal." His gaze drops to my lips, and he wets his own lips with his tongue. "It's really not."

I'm not sure if he's talking to me or himself, but he seems extremely fascinated with my lips.

Holy shit, is he going to kiss me again?

Holy shit, do I want him to kiss me again?

And while we're both sober?

Sober equals no excuses. Sober means we both want it.

Before I can decide what I'm going to do, the seesaw outside lets out an ear-scratching squeak and Kai and I both shudder.

"God, I think that just broke my eardrum." He presses his finger to his ear and works his jaw back and forth.

I free a trapped breath, relieved the noise happened and that it broke the intense moment. I honestly don't know what I would've done if Kai kissed me while we were sober. Part of me craves another taste of his soft lips again and the explosions I felt inside, while another part of me can't help but think of Kyler. Which means I shouldn't be kissing Kai.

I need to figure out what I want.

"We should probably get going," Kai says, gathering our trash, "if we're going to get you back in time for class."

"Yeah, we probably should." I climb out of the tree, taking my trash with me.

The walk back to school is quiet. I want to break the silence, because it's driving me crazy and makes me kinda sad—Kai and I never have awkward silence. But I don't know what to say to him, since I'm a little unclear on why he seems so standoffish. Was it because of the kiss? Or something else?

"So I'm going to a party tomorrow," he says to me as we turn and head up the path that leads to the entrance doors of the school. "I was thinking, if you wanted to, you could come with me."

"That sounds fun, and I really wish I could go." I really mean it. I wish I could go with him. "But . . . but I already told Kyler I'd go to his game."

"Oh, okay." Kai looks as perplexed as I feel.

I pick at a loose thread on the bottom of my dress as awkward silence stretches between us again. I hate this. I want to go back to our playful conversations. "Maybe if it gets over in time, I can meet up with you though," I say.

"Yeah, maybe." His forehead creases as he pulls open the door. "Are you driving with him? Or are you meeting him there?"

"He said I could ride with him . . . why?"

He shrugs as he holds the door open for me. "Just wondering if it's a date or not." He joins me in the hallway, letting the door go. "Sounds like a date to me, if he's picking you up." He grows quiet as he takes out his phone, glances at the screen, and chews on his bottom lip. "I have to go. I'll see you later, okay?" With that, he strides off down the hallway.

I watch him until he disappears around the corner, and then I head for my locker, my mind swimming in a sea of confusion, where nothing makes sense, not even myself, which is sadly becoming my motto in life.

I worked so hard to reinvent myself while I was on the trip, but I'm starting to realize the makeover was solely an outside thing. While I appear to be put together on the outside, I'm still as confused and lost as I was when I left.

Maybe even more.

Chapter
TWENTY-ONE

I spend the rest of the day stressing over how upset Kai looked when he left, but the second I walk into my house, my worries for Kai fly right out the window.

My dad is sitting at the kitchen table, drinking coffee and talking to Lynn about something while he reads over a piece of paper.

"Dad, you're home," I breathe in relief, wanting to get on my knees and kiss the ground. *Yes! I no longer have to do chores for Lynn and Hannah.*

But when he looks at me, my elation fizzles like flat soda. "We need to have a talk."

"What do you mean by *we*?" I ask. "You and me, or . . . ?" I glance at Lynn.

She twists in her chair and smiles sweetly. "Your father, me, and you are all going to talk." She pulls out a chair and pats the seat.

I hesitantly walk over to the table, dropping my bag on the floor before I take a seat in the chair farthest away from Lynn.

Her eyelids lower to slits, but she collects herself and reaches for the sugar dish in the middle of the table. "Your father and I are very worried about you, Isa." She scoops up a spoonful of sugar and adds it to her coffee. "Ever since you went on that trip, you've been acting like a completely different person."

"You wanted me to go on that trip," I calmly remind her.

A shrill laugh escapes her lips. "I never agreed that you could go on that trip. I was always under the impression that you were going to spend the summer at your grandmother's, getting a job and working so we would no longer have to spend so much money on you all the time."

My fingers curl inward as I ball my hands into fists. "I pay for most of my stuff." Which is the truth. Most of my pencils, sketchbooks, and clothes have come from money I've made doing part-time jobs here and there and from the cash my grandpa gave me.

"Stop lying." She stirs her coffee, sitting in the chair with perfect posture, trying to appear like the calm, picture-perfect woman she's not. "You've been doing too much of that lately."

"I haven't lied about anything," I say, fighting to keep my temper under control.

She wipes the spoon clean on the brim of the cup before setting it down on the table. "Maybe lying isn't the right word. But you've been keeping secrets from us."

I sort through my thoughts, trying to figure out which secret she's referring to.

"I'm talking about all the snooping you've been doing," she says. "For the last couple of weeks, you've torn this house apart every time your father and I aren't around."

I glance at the paper my dad was looking at when I walked in. It looks like a receipt from a hotel in Virginia, but it doesn't make any sense, since he was supposed to be in Florida. "How do you know I was looking for something?"

My dad must notice I'm looking, because he folds up the paper and stuffs it into his briefcase.

"I have my ways of finding out what you've been up to." Lynn's icy gaze warns me a storm is coming for me, and I'm not going to be able to get out of its path. "But that doesn't really matter. All that matters is that you found what you were looking for."

"I didn't find it." I feel like I'm walking into a trap. "Hannah left it on my bed, but I think you already know that, don't you?"

"Isabella, stop lying!" My dad suddenly explodes, slamming his fist onto the table.

I jump, my heart slamming against my chest. "Dad, I—"

"Don't you dare make excuses!" He cuts me off, stabbing a trembling finger in my direction. "You had no right to look for your birth certificate. No right at all."

"I do too have a right." I suck back the tears, refusing to cry in front of them. "It's *my* birth certificate. And when I turn eighteen in a few months, you would have had to give it to me anyway."

His face reddens with anger. "You don't even know what you're getting into. Just because you found out about *her*," he flinches, casting a panicked glance in Lynn's direction, "you think you understand everything."

"What I understand is that I was lied to for years. That the people I always thought were my family aren't. That this place," I flail my hand around at the kitchen, "wasn't always my home. That all these damn years I spent here, feeling like a fucking outcast, could've been avoided if you would've just let Grandma raise me, instead of bringing me into a family who hates me!" I'm breathing ravenously by the time I'm finished, but it feels so good to get it out.

The vein in my dad's forehead bulges as he glides his hand across the table and clutches my hand. "You will never talk to me that way again. Do you understand? I won't let you turn into your mother. I won't let you turn into that vile woman who ruined my life."

His fingers dig so violently into my hand I'm pretty sure I'm going to have bruises. "From now on, you will do everything Lynn and I tell you." He lets me go and pushes back from the table. "And as far as I'm concerned, she is your mother." He looks at Lynn before storming out of the kitchen.

"What did you think was going to happen?" Lynn says as I work to get oxygen into my lungs. "That he was going to tell you he was sorry and that deep down he really loved your mother?" She rolls her eyes at me when I say nothing.

"Your mother was a terrible person who did terrible things to people, and we've been trying to make it so you didn't end up like her." She scoots back from the table, looking at me with hatred as she grabs my hand and pulls me to my feet. "But from what I can see, you're going to end up just like her. Rotting in a grave that no one visits." She drags me with her as she heads for the doorway. "Now, you're going to come with me and paint over that god-awful painting you put up on that wall."

I can barely breathe. Barely think. Barely make sense of what she said.

My mom's a bad person?

She did terrible things?
I'm going to end up just like her?
She's dead?
I have to get out of here.

"No!" I shout, wrenching my hand from her hold. "I'm not going to paint that fucking wall. It's my wall. And I like the painting."

She doesn't seem shocked by my outburst. If anything, she seems pleased, like she's gotten everything she's wanted. "Just like your mother," she says.

I shove her, not enough to do much, but it still shocks her. Before she can say anything, I run out of the kitchen and down the driveway. I think about running to town or texting Grandma Stephy or Indigo to come get me, but before I can get that far, Kai appears at the corner of the sidewalk.

He starts to turn away the moment he spots me, but then he notices the tears in my eyes and rushes for me. "What's wrong?"

I shake my head. "I can't . . ." I suck in a huge breath of air. "I can't . . ." I start to sob hysterically and my legs buckle. "My mom's dead."

Kai catches me before I hit the ground and pulls me against his chest. I pull back, feeling moronic for having a meltdown in front of him, but he only presses me closer and lets me cry into his shirt.

"It's going to be okay," he says, smoothing his hand up and down my back. "I promise."

I wish he was right. I wish this was all a bad dream or something that I could eventually get over. Maybe one day I will. Maybe one day it won't hurt so badly. But right now, the pain is suffocating way more than the shell I used to live in, and I'm unsure how to make it go away or if it'll ever go away completely.

So I do the only thing I can do for now. I cry as hard as I can, letting it all out, grateful Kai is there to keep me from falling down completely.

Chapter
TWENTY-TWO

KAI

I don't know what to do to help her. All I know is that I wish I could take her pain away.

I've always had a soft spot for Isa ever since seventh grade, way before her girly makeover. But I fucked that friendship up by being a pussy and not standing up to my friends. I'm not like that anymore, though, haven't been for a while.

Over the last year, I've tried to become friends with Isa again, but every time I opened my mouth, she'd get pissed off. She's the only girl that's ever called me out on my bullshit, who's cared enough about me to ask if I'm okay, and one of the few girls who hasn't tried to use me to get to Kyler. And it pisses me off that he's trying to date her now. He didn't even give her the time of day until a few weeks ago, and he still has no clue what makes Isa so amazingly different from everyone else.

God, what I'd give to kiss her again, like I did in the driveway; only this time, we'd both be sober. I almost did it while we were in the tree, but I chickened out, because she hesitated. I know what that hesitation means. It means she didn't want to kiss me, and more than likely, she was probably thinking of Kyler.

Fucking story of my life.

"Kai, I think my mom's dead," Isa whispers.

Her face is still pressed to my chest, and it hurts like a bitch, because I'm pretty sure T broke a rib when he punched me earlier today. The punch was just the start of things if I can't come up with the money I owe him. Or that Bradon owes him anyway. Somehow, I got caught up in this fucking mess, because I stupidly vouched for Bradon, even though I knew I shouldn't. And now I'm the one T's coming after.

"Why do you think she's dead?" My fingers travel up and down Isa's back and my touch seems to soothe her.

"Lynn just told me she was." Her voice is hoarse. "She said she was a bad person and that she is rotting in her grave now."

I shake my head. Fucking Lynn. That woman is a bitch, just like her Mini Me Clone daughter. "Isa, you know Lynn could be lying to you? She's not a reliable source."

"Yeah, I know." She sniffles into my shirt. "But what if she's not lying? What if she's telling the truth?"

I think about the papers I tucked away in my back pocket about an hour ago, the papers Big Doug gave me from all the information he dug up on Isa's mom.

"But she might not be." I want to tell her what I

know, but I'm worried she'll completely break apart if I do it right now. Isa's a strong girl—she's had to be with all the shit she's put up with at home—but this is big. If I wait a few days, she'll be able to handle the news better, and that might give me enough time to get some more information on why her mom's in jail in Virginia. The papers said for murder charges, but didn't give all the details. I'm not buying the story yet. If there's one thing I've learned over the last couple of months, it's never assume things are what they appear to be.

"Why do your stomach muscles keep tightening?" she asks, pulling back to look at me. Her eyes are swollen and she's got the whole raccoon look going on, but she still looks beautiful. "Am I hugging you too hard?"

I snort a laugh. "Yeah, your tiny little arms are giving me booboos."

That gets her to smile, but then she instantly frowns as her eyes well up again.

"Hey, I have an idea." I drape my arm over her shoulders and steer her toward the house. "How about we go inside, get you some chocolate, and watch *Zombieland.*" I know she won't refuse, because sugar and zombies are the key to her heart.

"Thanks, Kai, you're such a good friend," she says, wiping her eyes with her sleeves. "Seriously, I don't know what I'd do without you."

My lip twitches at the friend reference, but I remind myself that it's for the best, at least until I get this shit with T sorted out, because the last thing I want to do is drag her into that mess. After that, though, all bets are off. That kiss in the tree will happen, but when she's ready.

She may think she likes Kyler, that he's the one for her, but she's wrong. Kyler doesn't get her like I do, doesn't know how to make her laugh, doesn't know how to talk comic book and superhero crazy talk with her like I do.

I just hope one day she realizes that.

Coming Soon

**THE YEAR OF FALLING IN LOVE
(ISABELLA ANDERS, #2)**

About the Author

Jessica Sorensen is a New York Times and USA Today bestselling author who lives in the snowy mountains of Wyoming. When she's not writing, she spends her time reading and hanging out with her family.

Connect with me online

jessicasorensen.com
and on
Facebook and Twitter

BOOKS BY

Jessica Sorensen

Isabella Anders Series:
The Year I Became Isabella Anders
The Year of Falling In Love (Coming Soon)

Unraveling You Series:
Unraveling You
Raveling You
Awakening You
Inspiring You

The Coincidence Series:
The Coincidence of Callie and Kayden
The Redemption of Callie and Kayden
The Destiny of Violet and Luke
The Probability of Violet and Luke
The Certainty of Violet and Luke
The Resolution of Callie and Kayden
Seth & Grayson

The Secret Series:
The Prelude of Ella and Micha
The Secret of Ella and Micha
The Forever of Ella and Micha
The Temptation of Lila and Ethan
The Ever After of Ella and Micha
Lila and Ethan: Forever and Always
Ella and Micha: Infinitely and Always

The Shattered Promises Series:
Shattered Promises
Fractured Souls
Unbroken
Broken Visions
Scattered Ashes

Breaking Nova Series:
Breaking Nova
Saving Quinton
Delilah: The Making of Red
Nova and Quinton: No Regrets
Tristan: Finding Hope
Wreck Me
Ruin Me

The Fallen Star Series (YA):
The Fallen Star
The Underworld
The Vision
The Promise

The Fallen Souls Series (spin off from The Fallen Star):
The Lost Soul
The Evanescence

The Darkness Falls Series:
Darkness Falls
Darkness Breaks
Darkness Fades

The Death Collectors Series (NA and YA):
Ember X and Ember
Cinder X and Cinder
Spark X and Cinder

The Sins Series:
Seduction & Temptation
Sins & Secrets
Lies & Betrayal (Coming Soon)

Unbeautiful Series:
Unbeautiful
Untamed

Standalones
The Forgotten Girl
The Illusion of Annabella

COMING SOON

Entranced
Steel & Bones
Forget Me Not (Sadie and Sage's story)
Iridescent (Fiona's story)

CPSIA information can be obtained at www.ICGtesting.com
Printed in the USA
LVOW11s2158170716

496704LV00004B/134/P